BLIND L…

Skye figured h… inside the cabi… …t of Skye's gun in the doorway, … …p of scalding coffee square in the Trailsman's face.

Blinded, Skye threw himself inside the cabin. Twisting and diving, he got off three hurried shots.

Through blurred vision, he saw one of his shots had hit the cast-iron stove and ricocheted, tearing into the bandit's back just as the man was about to shoot Skye down. Skye walked over and looked at the corpse, hoping it was Vicente Espinoza.

But the Trailsman had had his share of luck. It wasn't Espinoza, just one of the outlaw leader's men. And now Espinoza was alerted, ready to kill or be killed, and Skye Fargo knew he'd need both eyes and all his iron when he went up against the fastest gun that ever spat out death. . . .

THE TRAILSMAN 73

SANTA FE
SLAUGHTER

by
Jon Sharpe

A SIGNET BOOK

NEW AMERICAN LIBRARY

PUBLISHER'S NOTE

This book is a work of fiction. Names, characters, places, and incidents either are the product of the author's imagination or are used fictitiously, and any resemblance to actual persons, living or dead, events, or locales is entirely coincidental.

NAL BOOKS ARE AVAILABLE AT QUANTITY DISCOUNTS
WHEN USED TO PROMOTE PRODUCTS OR SERVICES.
FOR INFORMATION PLEASE WRITE TO PREMIUM MARKETING DIVISION.
NEW AMERICAN LIBRARY. 1633 BROADWAY.
NEW YORK. NEW YORK 10019.

The first chapter of this book previously appeared in *Calico Kill*, the seventy-second book in this series.

SIGNET TRADEMARK REG. U.S. PAT. OFF. AND FOREIGN COUNTRIES
REGISTERED TRADEMARK—MARCA REGISTRADA
HECHO EN CHICAGO. U.S.A.

SIGNET, SIGNET CLASSIC, MENTOR, ONYX, PLUME, MERIDIAN AND NAL BOOKS are published by NAL PENGUIN INC., 1633 Broadway, New York, New York 10019

First Printing, January, 1988

1 2 3 4 5 6 7 8 9

PRINTED IN THE UNITED STATES OF AMERICA

The Trailsman

Beginnings . . . they bend the tree and they mark the man. Skye Fargo was born when he was eighteen. Terror was his midwife, vengeance his first cry. Killing spawned Skye Fargo, ruthless, cold-blooded murder. Out of the acrid smoke of gunpowder still hanging in the air, he rose, cried out a promise never forgotten.

The Trailsman, they began to call him, all across the West: searcher, scout, hunter, the man who could see where others only looked, his skills for hire but not his soul, the man who lived each day to the fullest, yet trailed each tomorrow. Skye Fargo, the Trailsman, the seeker who could take the wildness of a land and the wanting of a woman and make them his own.

*July, 1861. In remote Santa Fe,
the mountain-rimmed capital of the
Territory of New Mexico, where intrigue
and suspicion are rampant. . . .*

1

Silent rage flowed across the table in mounting heated waves that Skye Fargo could almost feel, but he stayed calm as he stretched his long legs and settled back in his ornately carved wooden chair. Then he glared straight back at Cyrus Ashbrook.

"I know you've got plenty of problems, Mr. Ashbrook," Fargo said while toying with a toothpick, "but I didn't suspect that one of them was a hearing problem. Watch and listen real close here. My answer is no. N-O. Absolutely no. Definitely not. You've made it clear that taking the job means doing things your way. And when I work, I do things my way." Fargo paused to pick his teeth before concluding. "Do you understand me this time?"

All of Ashbrook's chins—at least three, although in the dim interior of a Santa Fe cantina, it was hard to get an exact count—started to quiver as his wispy white muttonchops bristled. The fleshy man had already drunk too much to be very civil. His beady bloodshot eyes glowed as he surveyed his three associates for reinforcement before returning to meet Fargo's icy visage.

But it was Chester Eakins, the gaunt man on Ashbrook's right, who pursued the appeal. He talked in a more reasonable and less imperious tone, rephrasing what Ashbrook had already said. "Mr. Fargo, it's like this. You know we're all merchants here in Santa Fe. We've got to have goods to sell, goods that come in by wagon train. Somebody's hitting our wagon trains on the way in, and sometimes even on the way out, even when all they've got aboard is that rough Mexican wool. It doesn't happen on every trip, but it happens often enough to where we can't hire crews."

"No, that's not quite right," interjected Josiah Watson, the dapper little man at the far right. "You can always hire crews—drifters, no-accounts, riffraff. Any of the good wagon men, though, can find all the work they want with other outfits. They're going around mean-mouthing us, saying that nobody in their right minds would work for us."

Fargo took in the cantina with his lake-blue eyes. This early in the evening, and with no recent wagon train arrivals or similar inducements to free spending, they were the only patrons. He spied the waitress emerging from the dark kitchen entrance, on her way to their table, before answering. "Likely the wagon men are right." he replied. "Nobody in his right mind would work for you. As best I know, I'm still in my right mind."

The waitress arrived at their massive round table and began picking up the remains of their dinner. Fargo gazed appreciatively at her as she removed his plate, especially enjoying the view when she bent to reach for an errant fork and revealed the substantial curvature that her low-cut blouse had advertised.

Her appearance reminded Fargo why he liked Santa Fe so much. In most other western towns, the women-folk tended to be pale, pinch-faced schoolmarms deter-mined to drain every ounce of pleasure out of life. As soon as they arrived, they agitated against saloons and gambling halls. They set up Sunday schools. They swooned when they heard someone say "leg." They wore at least four layers of clothes and felt violated if a man saw an ankle or elbow.

But the earthy women of New Mexico Territory weren't new arrivals bent on civilizing the heathens. They liked a good time just as much as the men did. They danced all night at fandangos in their gaudy scooped blouses and shamefully short skirts. They drank openly, right next to the men, while they laughed and flirted. They even smoked in public, not cigars like the men, but something they called *cigarrillos*—a pinch or two of tobacco rolled up in a cornhusk or leaf of paper torn out of an old Bible. The *señoritas* of Santa Fe never worried too much about what Queen Victoria might say, so they just enjoyed each day to the fullest.

In the cool of this evening in early July, with unspent coins jingling in his pocket, Fargo couldn't think of a better place to spend a few weeks. And he could think of some worse ways to pass time, such as scouring the desert along both sides of six hundred miles of Santa Fe Trail on a wild-goose chase, which was what these men had in mind.

Chester Eakins sported an immense beaklike nose that must have sniffed Fargo's thoughts. As soon as the waitress was out of earshot, he warily eyed everyone at the table and began speaking in a low and conspiratorial tone.

"Mr. Fargo, it's like this. Your search wouldn't be that difficult, because we know who's robbing our wagon trains. All you have to do is catch them. You're the Trailsman, the one who can track down anybody, so it should be easy once we tell you who's behind all this."

"And who might that be?" Fargo asked, settling into comfort with a good meal inside him and good beer in front of him. These men were stupid and disgusting, but not quite so disgusting that he felt any desire to stir.

Eakins glanced around again before leaning over to Fargo. "It's Russell, Majors, and Waddell. They're already the biggest freighting company in America, and they're fixing to get bigger. They're hitting our trains so they can drive all us little guys out of business. Then they'll have a monopoly on the Santa Fe trade."

Fargo slid his chair even farther back and began laughing so hard that he came close to falling out of his seat. "Jesus H. Christ," he exclaimed, catching his breath, "they're so big that you're not even a pimple on their ass."

Ashbrook leaned forward, knocking over his beer bottle. The amber liquid dripped back over his lap as he scowled at Fargo. "All right, Mr. Fargo, I can see that you don't believe what must be the truth. Who else could be hitting our wagon trains?"

"Who else?" Fargo asked, sitting up straight after his attack of laughter. "From here to Missouri, there's Indians: Comanche, Kiowa, Jicarilla Apache, Pawnee, Cheyenne, Osage, Kansa. They've all been known to bother wagons. Then there are the Comancheros, who don't do much else besides raid, rape, and plunder."

Ashbrook's grimace hadn't worked itself into a growl yet, so Fargo continued. "You've got a lot of Mexican folks around here who are still mad about the way things turned out back in 1846, and they figure it's their patriotic duty to pester gringos. Besides that, New Mexico Territory attracts hard cases and outlaws the way shit draws flies. I see pictures of your leading citizens hanging on the wall every time I go into a post office."

Before Ashbrook could interrupt, Fargo swigged the rest of his beer and concluded. "I don't take jobs unless I'm sure I can do them, and I don't see any way to do yours the way you want it done."

"Are you sure?" Ashbrook fumed as his three associates pretended to ignore the sloppy way the man grabbed Eakins' beer and got most of it on his linen shirt. "Could it be, Mr. Fargo, that you're a coward, that you're afraid to take a job that's right along your line?"

That was a piss-poor way to get somebody to hire on, Fargo thought, and a damn good way to get in a gunfight. But hell, he planned on staying awhile in Santa Fe, and it wasn't all that big a town. He couldn't count on never again seeing these shitheads and such friends as they might have, so he reined his impulse to teach Ashbrook some manners.

"Study on this for a minute," Fargo said. "The US Army shouldn't have anything to be afraid of out here, and they won't send anything less than a full cavalry troop into Comanche territory."

Zacharia Chandler, the round-faced man on Ashbrook's left, spoke for the first time since ordering dinner. He wore a starched white collar under his bushy black beard, and he looked odd. Most beards in mountain country grew full and haphazardly, but Chandler's was well-trimmed, and the man sported no mustache. The surrounding halo of hair made his face even rounder.

"Mr. Fargo, those troops are understandably reluctant to face the Comanche for their pittance of eighteen dollars a month. We are prepared to pay substantially more to stop these depredations."

Fargo wanted to laugh again, but maintained a stern expression as he signaled the waitress for some more beer. He looked around the table. "How long have you men been going back and forth, fetching goods in Missouri and selling them here?" Among the muttered answers, the longest was nine years.

"Then you might not have heard about what happened in the fall of '49, up at Point of Rocks, not too far over Glorieta Pass. Jim White was a merchant here, just like you, and he was on his way east. Jicarilla Apaches hit them there, killed all the men in the train. They rode off with Mrs. White and their little girl. She couldn't have been much more than eight or nine.

"Kit Carson and Antoine Leroux scouted for an army rescue party once word got back here. Took 'em nearly two weeks just to find the Indian camp. Before they could charge the camp, the Indians killed Mrs. White and then scattered, taking the little girl with them. The Whites had been fairly prominent folks, so the next year Congress voted a reward of fifteen hundred dollars to anyone who could bring the girl back."

Fargo held up and looked around to make sure they were still paying attention. "The point I'm getting to is this: fifteen hundred dollars in gold is a hell of a lot of money, more money than most men make in a year, more money than most men ever see in one pile. And there are too many men around here who'd stab their own mothers for five dollars, so you can imagine what they'd try for fifteen hundred gold dollars. It's been more than ten years since that reward was posted, and not one man has tried to earn it. Not one."

The Trailsman paused to moisten his throat with the dregs of his heavy, dark beer. "If the damn US government doesn't have enough money to persuade men to go poking around that godforsaken land of the Comanches and Apaches, you guys sure as hell don't either. God almighty doesn't have enough money to interest me in your damn wild-goose chase."

"Even Kit Carson didn't try?" Watson suavely asked. "From what I've read of him, he'd ride solo right into a Comanche camp to rescue the little girl."

"Old Kit's just flesh and blood like the rest of us," Fargo answered. He looked up to see the waitress with his beer. He saw two very pleasant aspects of her when she leaned over to fetch his empty, and they both seemed to enjoy the action.

Her smile vanished as soon as she straightened and rounded the table to see if the merchants wanted more beer. When she approached, the portly man slid his chair back, blocking her way. With surprising agility for a man so fat and slobbering drunk, his arms found their way around her small waist. Fargo got a tantalizing glimpse of smooth mahogany thigh when her skirt fluttered up while Ashbrook pulled her down onto his lap.

Flabbergasted, she wiggled while Ashbrook moved an uncallused hand up under her skirt, his other holding her firmly by a breast. "Why smile at him, sweetie, when I could show you a real good time?"

She wiggled some more and hissed as the fat man's hand moved upward. Fargo glanced around the table; Ashbrook's companions were acting as though the man amid them was a total stranger, someone they'd never seen before and hoped never to see again.

"Come on, girlie. What's it going to cost me for a little roll in the hay?"

"I am not some *puta*," the girl spat, her put-up tresses coming loose to cascade over her bare shoulders in a flood of sable grandeur. The vermilion rose that had adorned her hair fluttered to the floor as she writhed, unable to escape Ashbrook's grasp. "I do not sell myself to men, especially rich gringos who think they can buy anything they see. Let me go, you *perro*."

Her efforts energized Ashbrook, even when she brought a hand around and clawed at his sweaty face. "All you hot-blooded little spitfires are alike," he announced, "and you all want the same thing. So let's stop playing games.

I've been jerked around enough tonight by people that say they're not interested when I know they really are."

She wrenched while Ashbrook spoke, a swift move that broke his hold on her right breast. The fat man's stubby hand clutched her blouse as she continued to wriggle; the thin cloth ripped, exposing her delectable bosom, firm full breasts crowned by cherry-sized chocolate nipples.

Fargo had seen enough. Not enough of the waitress, certainly, but what he'd seen of Ashbrook was more than enough to give him a sour taste in his mouth. Not that Ashbrook's more sedate associates were much better as they stared at the ceiling or floor, trying to pretend that they were somewhere else. Cyrus Ashbrook was their dog, but they weren't about to call him off.

The slim waitress had sidled so that Fargo now faced Ashbrook's bulging right side while the rotund man's eager hands were pawing away. As he sprang to his feet, Fargo shoved on the heavy table. It was much too ponderous to slide more than a foot or so, not far enough to poke Ashbrook's belly. It stopped, but the bottles continued to slide, four of them right into Ashbrook.

The startled merchant, his beady eyes alternating between the tumbling glass and the bared bosom, didn't even feel the presence behind him until a muscular, scarred arm locked around his neck. The sudden presence jammed his Adam's apple toward his spine and began cutting off his air. Slowly his right hand fell from the girl's chest and his left emerged from the skirt.

The girl gazed up at Fargo with appreciative brown eyes, her long lashes fluttering. Fargo grinned and nodded. Only when she finally took her eyes off him did she realize she was half-undressed. With a dusky blush that started near her toes and worked up, she gasped, crossed her arms over her beautiful bust, turned, and dashed back to the kitchen.

Releasing his pressure on Ashbrook's neck, Fargo jerked on a handful of wispy muttonchop whisker to wrench the man around so he could see his flushed face.

"You just can't learn to take no for an answer, can you?" Ashbrook tried to avoid facing Fargo's pitiless stare, but the Trailsman pulled his head back around. "I'd rip your head off right now, but you're so much like a goddamn worm that both ends of you would grow back, and then the world would be stuck with two of you."

Fargo glared down at the lard-faced merchant. "I don't know what she'd have to do to change your mind when you get set on something. But I'll do whatever it takes." Fargo pushed Ashbrook's head down and around to face the others.

All three of the men seemed to have noticed something amiss with their boots, for they were all staring downward with great intensity. "And you. Yeah, you, Chester Eakins. And you, Josiah Watson. And you, Zacharia Chandler. Every one of you was more than willing to sit there while your half-drunk friend and business associate here tried to rape some gal right in front of you. Not one of you so much as said a word, let alone lifted a hand in her defense."

It was Chandler, the quiet one, who dared to answer. "Mr. Fargo, we're all men of the world here. You need not pretend that Carmelita is some innocent maiden."

"I don't care if she's the easiest lay this side of the Mississippi," Fargo shot back. "She made it real clear that this lard-bucket Ashbrook wasn't in her plans for tonight. The way I see it, two people sharing a bed is something they both ought to be agreed on."

Fargo realized he should have stopped there, but his anger wouldn't let him. "You're all respectable, responsible businessmen, so you say, and you let this happen right in front of you. You say Cyrus Ashbrook is your trusted associate, and he can't even rely on you to keep him from making a fool out of himself. I can't work for people I don't trust, and if you betray one of your own little crowd, just how much confidence could I have in you?"

With that, Fargo stomped out the cantina door. He didn't want anyone to see him and think that he was the sort of man who'd sit at the same table as those dimwits.

Once outside, Fargo's rage was dissipated by his pounding footsteps that thudded into the dusty street, and cooled by the evening air at the western foot of the Sangre de Cristo Mountains. His disposition had improved markedly when he turned a corner, ready to leave the plaza area and head down toward the seedier part of town that held his rented room.

Across the street, a glimmer of light caught Fargo's eye. He stepped back into the shadows to watch as the glimmer became a slit, and then an open doorway. His eyes adjusting quickly to the brightness, Fargo saw gaming tables attended by men in hammer-prong frock coats and women in breathtaking silken gowns. As a couple approached the door to leave, a hack appeared from around the corner and pulled up, its timing precise as clockwork.

This must be it, Fargo thought, the famous Palace Club. Everyone had heard of it, but the only people who got in were the wealthy and the well-connected.

Fargo couldn't help but feel curious about the place, and he was about as well-dressed now as he ever planned to get before his funeral. Straightening the tie he had worn for his meeting with the businessmen, Fargo crossed the street and tapped on the thick wooden door.

The doorman admitted Fargo and shunted him into a small side room. "This is a private club, sir, open only to members and guests." Fargo might have had an inch on the man in height, but the fellow more than made up for that in the shoulder department. He wasn't likely to get many arguments, and Fargo didn't feel like starting one. Instead, the Trailsman told as much truth as seemed reasonable.

"Of course I know that," Fargo replied calmly, "I learned of this establishment when I was in San Francisco recently on business."

"I see." The doorman nodded. "Could you give any references? Could you tell me who you are, what your business is, perhaps?"

The Trailsman nodded agreeably and spoke slowly, picking his words with care. "My last name is Fargo. You ought to be able to surmise the rest. Discretion forbids me from disclosing any more about why my business has brought me to New Mexico."

By tomorrow morning, Fargo knew, there would be talk all over town that Wells Fargo was planning to extend its express and stagecoach services to New Mexico Territory. Why else would a member of the wealthy Fargo family of San Francisco be visiting Santa Fe?

In truth, Skye Fargo had taken his name from the company, not the other way around. The memories pained him, gnawed at him. His father had been a Wells Fargo agent until their home was raided, the entire family brutally massacred. Away at the time, only the son escaped the butchery. He vowed vengeance and an eternal search for the culprits, and took the name Fargo.

Forcing those atrocious memories out of his consciousness, Skye Fargo acknowledged the doorman's nod, checked his ludicrous plug hat, and entered the front room. Its opulence was almost blinding. Two great chandeliers hung from the high ornate ceiling; plush Turkish carpets covered much of the polished hardwood floor. Gaming tables—baccarat, roulette, billiards, craps—lined three mahogany walls; the fourth side was dominated by an immense bar. Perhaps fifty people, all dressed to the nines, were enjoying themselves. It reminded Fargo of the grand salon of a luxurious Mississippi River steamboat, except it was even fancier.

Farther back, Fargo soon discovered, was another room, not quite as big or plush. There men sat in soft leather chairs and played poker, thousands of dollars changing hands every night. Uncertain as to whether he'd have to sign for his drink or just pay on the spot for it when the double shot of bourbon arrived, Fargo ordered from the backroom waiter and watched the action.

Only one table was busy, with eight or nine men quietly playing seven-card stud. Twenty feet across the room, far enough away so that they couldn't be accused of kibitzing, stood four onlookers, all men. Apparently the ladies stayed in the front room here. Fargo gravitated toward the bystanders, who were friendly enough.

"Lord Cavendish is winning big again," one commented. Another added, "For a limey that says he always played whist before touring the West, he plays some smart poker. If he stays in town much longer, he'll clean it out."

"Excuse me, fellows," Fargo interjected. "I'm new in town and haven't heard of Lord Cavendish. Which one is he?"

"The sandy-haired one with his back to us and that huge pile of chips at his side. That's His Most Gracious Excellency, Percival Oliver Stanley Cavendish, Fourth Earl of Barrington."

"I see," Fargo replied, keeping his eyes on Lord Cavendish. Something about the man looked familiar, and Fargo's suspicions were confirmed when the lean man turned, his aristocratic features acknowledging Fargo's presence with a wink and a wince. Then Cavendish returned his attention to raking in another pot. He shuffled, waited for the cut, and began to deal.

The last time Fargo had seen Lord Cavendish, the man had been known as Perk Doyle, a common sight along the riverfront saloons of Saint Louis when he was afloat on a paddle-wheeler. Like most professional gamblers, Perk Doyle never really gambled. He always bet sure things. With his nimble hands, Doyle was talented at converting games of chance into sure things.

Such enormous success as Lord Cavendish had been enjoying in Santa Fe could hardly be attributed to beginner's luck.

"I want another deal." The voice, low and menacing, came from the dark-featured man directly across the table from Lord Cavendish, sitting so that Fargo had a good view of him.

"Why would that be, my good man?" Cavendish asked innocently. "I don't recall dropping any cards or otherwise causing what you Americans call a misdeal."

"Cut the bullshit." The man's brows beetled. "I've been watching close. That last card you dealt yourself didn't come off that top of the deck. You've been rigging deals all week."

"Indeed." Cavendish looked around the table. "Do you other men believe I misdealt? I shall be glad to deal again if you so wish."

"Can't you understand me?" the aggrieved man roared, rising from his chair. "I'm saying you're cheating at cards. What're you going to do about it?"

19

Cavendish slowly shrugged, moving the man's attention to his shoulders while his adroit hands started to palm a derringer from a vest pocket. Fargo could tell that Cavendish was primed, ready to shift his position instantly.

His husky antagonist brought up a revolver. "I think it's time we settled this, you highborn cardshark." Cavendish instantly rolled under the table, too fast for his poker victim to perceive. One shot rang out and drilled into the thick wooden floor.

Confused, the man looked up to see Skye Fargo watching the show. "What're you standing there for, grinning like a shit-eating hound?" Enraged, the man grabbed the edge of the felt-covered table with his free hand and jerked it upward, tilting it back so violently that it tipped over. The edge came down hard on Lord Cavendish, stunning him and pinning his slender legs to the floor.

"You limey weasel," the man bellowed as the other poker players scattered, "you'll never cheat me again." With both shaky hands on the grip, he bore the revolver down on the immobilized Lord Cavendish.

"Don't do that," Fargo barked. The man's thick eyebrows rose as he lifted his hateful stare from Cavendish to the Colt that had just emerged from beneath Fargo's borrowed frock coat.

"You're going to stay out of this." He brought up his own revolver to make sure Fargo stayed out of it.

By now convinced that anyone who had money in Santa Fe lacked even a spoonful of brains, Fargo fired his own gun. The slug caught the man where his eyebrows came together, slamming first his head backward, then his neck, followed by his torso.

Before the man toppled to the floor, Fargo had leapt across the room. He wrenched the table off Cavendish and pulled the ersatz lord up on his feet, then waltzed him out the back exit Fargo had spotted earlier. No one seemed too eager to follow them, so they had the alley to themselves as Lord Cavendish leaned against the adobe back wall to catch his breath.

"You saved my ass in there, Fargo." Stately Lord Cavendish had dropped his London accent to talk like grateful Perk Doyle. "I owe you one."

"You owe me more than that. I can think of about three hundred things you owe me, which is why I pulled you out of there. Collecting old bills from a corpse can be a lot of work, as you likely know. Tonight wasn't the first time you've doctored a deck."

In the blue light of the waxing sliver of a moon, Doyle's chiseled features furrowed. "Oh, yeah, that. Down by New Orleans, wasn't it? You just happened to be sitting at the wrong table, Fargo, that's all. I wasn't after your money. It was that loudmouth Alabama planter I was fixing to skin. But you've got to set things up, work them around, before you can clean up big. You'd have got your three hundred dollars back before the night was over. Wasn't my idea to have the game end early when that damn steamboat's boiler blew up."

Doyle paused and reached into his pocket, bringing up a fistful of twenty-dollar gold pieces. "Here, Fargo. If it's not enough, let me know."

"I will." Fargo nodded and stuck the money into his own pockets. "Now, you think you can buy me a drink somewhere while you explain how Perk Doyle the riverboat gambler became Percival Cavendish, the fourth earl of Barrington?"

Over a bottle of eight-year-old malt whiskey in his suite at the La Fonda Hotel, Doyle told the story.

"Was back in Saint Louis last spring, up to my usual trade, when I got in a game at a fancy hotel. They were pretty high-toned folks, so I didn't cheat any more than they did. I wanted to get the feel of things before setting any of them up. Anyway, one of 'em was visiting from England with a passel of servants, and he asked me if I'd ever been out West."

Fargo settled back into the overstuffed chair and nodded as he poured himself another drink of the smooth whiskey. "Well, had you?"

"Once. Out to California and back. But there's people along the Overland Trail that have long memories, and I reckon it's better for my health if I don't return. But I told the man I had gone West once, and he said I was a likable chap and he needed to hire a guide to New Mexico. Seems he was pretty well off himself, and his friends were even richer. He was the front man for a British syndicate that planned on putting together some huge cattle operations in Texas and New Mexico.

"So I hired on as his guide. Not much more'n a fortnight out of Council Grove, out by Pawnee Rock, the son of a bitch up and died on us. Might have been Arkansas River water that fetched him, or the alkali dust clouds, or maybe he just had a weak ticker. Anyway, he just turned sickly one night, and the next morning he was dead."

"And he was His Most Gracious Excellency, Percival Oliver Stanley Cavendish, Fourth Earl of Barrington," Fargo surmised.

"You got it," Doyle said, pulling out a penknife to cut off the tip before lighting a long fragrant Havana cigar.

Following a few puffs to make sure it would stay lit, Doyle finished the story. "His servants weren't in any hurry to go back to England, where everybody treated 'em like shit. They liked our wide-open spaces and our wide-open society, and they agreed with me that Lord Cavendish could have just as easy died on the trip back as on the trip out. So we all decided I'd be Lord Cavendish for a spell. It's done wonders for my career. You know how much easier it is to get into a high-stakes game when everybody thinks you're some well-feathered British pigeon waiting to be plucked?"

Fargo leaned back and laughed. "I'll be damned. Speaking of that, you got any idea who it was I had to kill tonight?"

A frown implanted itself on Doyle's face. "Hector MacIver. Cattleman with a big spread south of here, down on the Rio Hondo. Kind of testy."

"I noticed," Fargo responded. "He have any friends I should know about?"

"Not worth mention," Doyle said, pulling on the cigar. "He was surly all the time I saw him, and talk was that if there was an Asshole Association around here, MacIver would have been its president. He was rich and well-connected, but I don't think anybody's going to miss him. Might have had a bodyguard, most of those big ranchers bring a gunhand along whenever they come to the territorial capital. But the Palace Club doesn't admit such riffraff, and that's the only place I ever saw MacIver."

Fargo poured another drink while Doyle continued. "The main reason he got so proddy about the way I handled cards is that he'd pulled the same trick a few hands back when he dealt. When I finally called him, he was sure he had my bluff beat. He didn't do a very good job of hiding his surprise when I turned over my cards and they weren't what he'd dealt me."

Pursuing this any farther would mean inquiring into Doyle's professional secrets, especially the patent sleeve rig under the man's silk shirt that could push selected cards into a man's hand without attracting notice. Bidding Perk Doyle *adiós*, Fargo made his own way out of the La Fonda and again started toward his rented room, planning on a quiet night's sleep.

Keeping to the shadows as he made his way along San Francisco Street, Fargo left the huge cathedral behind and entered the more ragged part of town. As he passed another of the one-room adobe houses that sat amid goats and chicken, he heard a hiss.

"Ven aca, señor." The throaty whisper came from a door that was just cracked open. In this part of town, Fargo knew, white men had been murdered for their boots, let alone the four hundred or so dollars he was carrying. He dropped instantly to the ground, rolled fast, and had his Colt aimed at the voice.

He felt a little foolish a moment later when a high-pitched giggle came through the thin bracing air.

"Señor Fargo, it is I, Carmelita. *Por favor*, do not shoot at me."

This wouldn't be the first time that a pretty gal's voice had led Fargo into trouble, so he remained wary as he stood up and lowered the pistol.

"Quick, Señor Fargo, step inside."

He could barely make out which of the shadows in the doorway was her face as he stepped toward it, his eyes darting around the moonlit street.

Inside the tiny building, it was darker than the inside of a cow, a problem Carmelita solved with a tallow candle. "Señor Fargo, you saved me from that pig," she

23

explained. Fargo had trouble concentrating on her voice, because she was wearing a brief cotton shift that left precious little to the imagination. "So I must repay you."

She motioned for him to sit beside her on the bright striped blankets that covered the bed, virtually the only furniture in the room. Fargo obliged, savoring the musky scent as she sidled next to him.

"After you left, the cantina got busy. Later there was much talk of the shooting at the Palace Club."

Fargo would have sworn that it was impossible for her smooth thigh to press any tighter against his, but somehow she managed.

"One man at the cantina, he was big and ugly, he said Señor MacIver is his *patrón* and he must avenge Señor MacIver. He found out they think man named Fargo killed Señor MacIver. He said he knows where this Fargo man is staying, so he will ambush him there. After he left, I asked who Fargo is." She paused just long enough to sigh and twist slightly, making Fargo achingly aware of her luscious breasts, the erect dark nipples clearly outlined through the white cotton shift.

She went on talking, though. "He is the man who helped me before I had to push a knife into Señor Ashbrook's back. I watched for you to tell you."

Reasonably certain that MacIver's bodyguard had not started looking for a new job quite yet, Fargo hadn't exactly planned on hiring a brass band and leading the parade when he returned to his rented room. But it was mighty thoughtful of Carmelita anyway, and if he was any judge of the smoke signals coming from her glistening dark eyes and long fluttering lashes, she wasn't quite finished with her repayment.

Fargo kept his hands in his lap. He wanted Carmelita, wanted her so bad that he'd walk funny for a week just thinking about her. But he had a feeling, deep in his gut, that he'd best hold back.

"Are we even now, Señor Fargo? You saved me from that pig, and I warned you about that man's plan to kill you?"

Fargo forced himself to stand and get across the small

room, his steps silent on the dirt floor, before turning to face Carmelita, her legs now drawing his attention, the pleasing way her calves turned, how the shift didn't even reach her knees, the barely hidden delights that must be waiting atop those sleek thighs.

"You never did owe me anything, Carmelita," Fargo heard himself say. "I only did what any man there should have done. You've thanked me enough." The room had a back door, and Fargo had his suspicions. "Might you excuse me for a moment?"

Without waiting for her answer, Fargo spun and kicked the flimsy back door open. It didn't open more than a foot or so, so Fargo kicked it again, even harder, and this time he heard the satisfying impact of wood slamming into a rib cage. Then he heard something heavy fall to the dirt, followed by a moan of pain. Fargo added to the pain a moment later when the man, as big and ugly as advertised, made the mistake of reaching for his pistol and got the full force of Fargo's booted weight on his hand.

The shriek back in the house most likely represented yet another effort by a not-too-skilled actress, so Fargo ignored it and bent over, grabbing a shock of greasy hair and jerking the man's head up. "You feel like explaining just why my nightlife is so interesting to you?"

The man groaned and rolled his head. Between the moon and the bit of candlelight that came through the door, Fargo could see the scarred face of a man who'd been around. Around too many times. A patch covered his left eye, the man's lopsided nose had been broken at least twice, the top of his ear had been bitten off, and the man's mouth, which gaped every time he wheezed in a labored breath, did not hold anything close to a full set of teeth.

But his good eye held hatred, aimed at Fargo. After catching his breath, he stiffened his back and sat up straight. "You know why I'm after you. You killed my boss, you asshole."

"I don't know what you heard of it, but I didn't have too much goddamn choice in the matter." Fargo knelt, his pistol ready in case the man forgot who was in charge.

"Don't matter how I heard it. Hector was for certain a mean-ass shitheel. No doubt in my mind he had it comin'. He's had it comin' for a long time. But I owed him that much."

"Why might that be?" Fargo heard stirrings in the adobe. The shadows shifted, indicating the flickering tallow candle was approaching, borne by the most alluring and perhaps the most treacherous womanflesh he'd encountered for some time. The last thing the Trailsman wanted to worry about right now was his back.

"Carmelita, honey," he intoned without turning, "best you stay inside.

"Now, where were we?" Fargo asked. "Oh, yeah. You were fixing to explain just why you owed it to Hector to come after me."

"He give me a job when nobody else'd have me, that's why. Man's gotta work, you know an' it's hard to be too damn choosy when you're me. Ain't like there's a big line of men waitin' to put me on the payroll. But Hector did, an' he never did give me no shit about the way I look."

"Yes," Fargo conceded, "I can see why you owed Hector. Well, you came goddamn close, setting me up with that hot-blooded little *señorita* the way you did. Hell, she could have lured Bishop Lamy into bed, and I for damn sure never took no vow of eternal chastity."

The man came up with a laugh. "She wasn't in on it, Fargo. When you didn't show up at your room like I figured you should, I come back this way. I seen you comin' up the street, an' I took cover. Was gonna take care of you when you come by, but then you come in here. So I kind of tagged along."

Fargo stood, and so did the husky man. "You got a name?"

"Ugly Jack. One-Eyed Jack. Bottle-Nose Jack. Gouge-Ear Jack. Gap-Tooth Jack. Mebbe some others that folks don't say where I can hear."

"Jack's enough. Listen, Jack." Fargo leaned into the man's face. "You can't work for Hector MacIver anymore because he isn't around to pay you. And if you ever try fucking with me again, you'll have a full-time job that'll last forever. You'll be pushing up daisies. That clear?"

Jack nodded. "I catch your drift, Fargo."

"Good. You know where the Ashbrook warehouse is?"

"Not exactly. This here's my first time in Santa Fe. El Paso's my home stomping grounds. Or used to be."

"Never mind. The warehouse is on the south side of the plaza. Just ask around. I don't think you'll have a bit of trouble finding some work over there."

Fargo felt the chill of late night in the high country sink into him as he watched Jack turn and plod away into the eerie moonlight that made these humble mud houses shimmer like silver-plated palaces. An even deeper chill penetrated when he realized it was time to go back inside and deal with Carmelita.

2

Warily, Fargo stepped back into the one-room adobe house, his Colt drawn in case Carmelita should come at him with weapons more substantial, but probably less lethal, than her abundant feminine wiles.

The stubby candle still flickered atop the warming shelf above her compact cast-iron cook stove. Fargo didn't know whether to be relieved or disappointed that its wavering light showed that Carmelita had fled. Her shoes, which had been sitting on the clay floor next to a bedpost, had vanished. An outfit was missing from the row of clothes that hung on wooden pegs driven into the earthen wall. Moonlit tracks out the front door, made by a short fast-stepping woman, provided further confirmation.

This was just about the last place where anyone with a grudge was likely to look for him tonight, Fargo decided. He gratefully undressed and crawled into Carmelita's bed.

Her cot wasn't very comfortable, given the way the needlelike stuffing was bent on working its way out of the straw mattress and digging into Fargo's back. Besides that, the bed's frame was no match for Fargo's, so he couldn't stretch fully to relax. He kept thinking he might accidentally bite his kneecaps once he fell asleep, but quickly accepted that risk.

By the gray light of dawn, just as the sun began its daily climb over the Sangre de Cristos, Fargo felt another presence in the room. Instantly alert, his eyes mere slits of vigilance as he forced his breathing to mimic the patterns of sleep, he took in the room.

He wanted to pinch himself and make sure he wasn't still dreaming. Carmelita stood between the bed and the stove, looking down at Fargo while sultry expressions played across her round face. She sighed with what sounded like anticipation, then hoisted the blouse, casting it across the room.

Pretending to be asleep got even harder when she undid the cotton rope belt that held up the skirt. That wasn't all that got harder. Fargo could feel his pole lifting the rough wool blankets. Carmelita turned to face the stove, and Fargo enjoyed another aspect of her splendid physique. He wanted those firm round buttocks in his hands just as much as he desired her sleek thighs to envelop him, as much as he hungered for those majestic breasts.

The faintest sound of metal against metal ended Fargo's romantic reverie. He recalled that there had been a long and well-honed butcher knife up on the warming shelf, next to the candle.

He also recalled that women weren't always friendly, even when they acted that way. In these parts, it was not unknown for a *señorita* to lure a man into bed. Once she was all wrapped around him, she could reach over, grab a knife, and plant it in his back. He couldn't figure out why Carmelita might have that in for him, but after last night's back-door run-in with Ugly Jack, Fargo didn't see any reason to go out of his way to trust Carmelita.

In the blink of an eye, Fargo rolled out of the short bed and sprang up behind Carmelita, his huge hands pinning her arms. Something clattered down onto the stovetop. What she seemed to notice, though, was the force of his throbbing manhood against the small of her back.

"Oh, Señor Fargo," she gasped. "How could you know how much I love to do it this way, standing up?"

No matter how strong his suspicions about Carmelita's motivations, Fargo didn't see much way they could have anything except fun if her hands stayed on the stove.

She shifted her stance, her feet moving apart as she arched back at Fargo. Feeling momentary twinges from his night of cramped sleeping, Fargo bent his knees sufficiently to resolve their difference in heights. Using her delectable breasts for handles to make sure he stayed in line, Fargo plunged ahead, enjoying every moment as her tight moistness consumed the sensitive tip of his shaft.

Leisurely rocking forward and back, Carmelita slowed Fargo's penetration to tiny increments as he felt her nipples swell and then push outward through the gaps between his bowed fingers. Gaining only a little on each sway, Fargo at first felt tense, desperate to drive deeper.

But what's the hurry to move on? he asked himself. It isn't like you don't enjoy what you're doing now.

After that, he took his deepening pleasures as they came to him, increment by tantalizing increment. She would allow another minuscule gain, then rotate, her jutted buttocks just grazing Fargo's sensitized pubis. Then she would slide forward, ever so slowly, squeezing Fargo's pulsating staff until it was expelled into the cold, dry morning air.

With inerrant accuracy, Carmelita's dewy depths would return to again find Fargo and take him in for another unhurried exploration of her chamber of mutual pleasure.

Outside, it must have been close to daylight, for Fargo could discern every peak and trough along her flexed backbone, her glistening brown skin moving in a rhythm that he matched perfectly, thrust for thrust. All he could see of her was her back and a bobbing head of straight black hair.

"Ahora," she pleaded, *"ahora mismo."* Fargo's knowledge of border Spanish was a little rusty, but he had a fair idea what she had in mind. Giving her a taste of her own leisurely timing, he slowly slid his cupped hands from her breasts, pausing to savor the feverish expansion and contraction of her rib cage beneath his fingertips. His progress again halted near her navel for a gentle massage of her taut midriff, eventually descending and spreading until he had a padded hipbone firmly in each hand.

Then the Trailsman pulled himself into her, forcing ever inward and upward.

Her back arched like a startled cat's. *"Eres un toro,"*

she cried. Fargo could feel her thighs tighten as she rose to her tiptoes and fingertips, and he kept pushing, penetrating, knowing they had a ways to go yet.

Launching himself like a Fourth of July skyrocket, Fargo surrounded his yearning shaft with her satisfying moist warmth. Her fingertips rose from the stove as she straightened, settling more firmly astride Fargo.

"*Dios, mío*" she exclaimed, gasping, and Fargo kept her gasping as he straightened his knees, lifting her feet from the floor, a position they held as spasm after spasm of fulfillment erupted from Fargo to explode deep inside an ecstatic, writhing Carmelita.

Once matters settled down a little and Carmelita noticed how light it was getting to be outside, she broke off, explaining why she'd been so scared that she ran off last night to stay with a friend.

Maybe it all really had happened the way she and Ugly Jack had both said it had, but Fargo still wasn't about to put Carmelita anywhere near the top of his list of trustworthy people. Intrigues ran deep here, sometimes too deep to fathom, and her explanations seemed too pat.

"You must hurry on now, Señor Fargo," she said, pulling on her flimsy cotton shift. "My neighbors do not like to think that one of our kind entertains one of your kind."

Fargo nodded. All through the Southwest, the Mexican folks complained that they got a raw deal from the Anglos, that the Anglos were hostile and bigoted. But the Mexicans were no less hostile and bigoted than the Anglos. There were many Anglos that got riled at the thought of a brown-skinned man anywhere near a pale-skinned woman, and damn near as many hot-blooded *hombres* that would kill any white man they thought was trifling with one of their womenfolk.

Fargo's jet-black hair and dark features, including the high cheekbones of some Cherokee ancestors, might have allowed him to pass unnoticed in this neighborhood at night. But in broad daylight, his size and blue eyes would give him away instantly. He dressed while the roosters crowed outside.

But he got out her door and a ways down the dusty

street without attracting attention from anything more than a few curious goats. He stopped to get his bearings. One winding street looked pretty much the same as any other here, and he wanted to head straight for his rented room without walking any farther than he had to. Between last night's cramped bed and the way he'd had to keep his knees bent this morning, his aching legs sure didn't need a workout.

He turned and spied the twin towers of the cathedral back by the plaza. Glancing over at the mountains to the east, he noticed that any minute now, the sun would pop up. It was later than he'd thought, but he really didn't have much to do today.

Confident that his room lay only a few blocks ahead, Fargo strolled down the street, raising little clouds of dust with each step. He paid little mind to a trim phaeton carriage coming his way, drawn by a matched pair of high-stepping bays.

It halted right next to him. A tall woman in drab gray hoopskirts removed her gloved hand from the brake, and within the shadow of the black top, Fargo could make out a few blond curls creeping out from under her somber wide-brimmed traveling hat. Her voice was crisper than the morning air.

"I should have thought, Mr. Fargo, that you of all men would have better taste."

"You can think whatever you want, honey," Fargo replied, wishing that she'd save her moralizing lectures for the next session of the sewing circle or temperance league.

"Imagine," she huffed, "imagine that one of the Fargos was seen consorting with the rabble. It was bad enough for a man of your means and upbringing to be drawn into gunplay over a game of chance, but this . . . What are things coming to?" Her words were those of an old biddy, but the timbre of her voice struck Fargo differently.

"I can't say, honey, but I can tell you where I'm going to. On up the street." Her face was just too shadowed for Fargo to estimate her age, and his knees were telling him that they'd rather do something besides stand still in the street. He resumed his walk.

"Please wait a moment, Mr. Fargo." Fargo didn't, but he did hear her say, "Since you seem determined to go somewhere, might I offer you a ride?"

After climbing into the carriage and getting his eyes adjusted to the shade, Fargo saw that he was with a young woman, not much past twenty. "Is it fair to ask what made you change your mind about my depraved morals and ask me aboard?"

She released the brake and shook the reins before answering. "Mr. Fargo, I know who you are and why you are here. I saw you in the Palace Club last night."

Fargo tried to remember just which one of the begowned and bejeweled she might have been. Sure, a young tall blonde had been in the front hall, standing amid a small gathering near the roulette table. He hadn't caught much more than a glimpse, though. He told her that he'd seen her there, too, so that she'd go on.

"San Francisco is well-known for being open-minded," she said, "but Santa Fe is different."

She slowed to take a corner, in order to go around a block and get the phaeton pointed the way Fargo had been heading. That was about the only practical way for a woman to get a carriage turned around. The streets weren't wide enough to loop around in. Backing a carriage required more control than most people had over their horses. In a pinch, a man could undo the pulls, turn the carriage around by human muscle, and then walk the team around and reattach them. But that was more than most women felt up to.

"Just how is Santa Fe different?" Fargo asked, admiring how well the phaeton was sprung. Riding a cheap buckboard across ruts like these would rattle your teeth, but this ride was smooth.

"I know you're here on business for your family's company," she said, her voice growing less strident. "And I desperately want you to succeed. Santa Fe is so cut off, so isolated, from the rest of the world, from Saint Louis and New York and all the important places."

"It is a ways from here to anywhere else," Fargo conceded as the next corner appeared and she ignored it and went straight on.

"Once you complete your negotiations and we have regular Wells Fargo service here, we won't be at the mercy of that dreadful Butterfield Stage Company. Their service is sporadic at best. Important news arrives late. Fashions are years out of date by the time they arrive in New Mexico. Civilized people are afraid to visit."

"I'm sure the Butterfield folks do the best they can," Fargo replied, noticing that she'd missed another chance to turn around. There wouldn't be too many more, because they were now on the edge of town, almost into the foothills where scattered stands of aspen waved their pale leaves in the almost imperceptible breeze.

"I knew you were at heart a gentleman," she answered, steering the carriage to avoid a foot-high rock in the road. "You know your own company is superior, so you feel no need to demean your competitors."

Fargo murmured agreement that gentlemen did indeed behave that way, and listened to her continued explanation.

"As I said, it is very important that Wells Fargo serve Santa Fe. But the important men, the men who decide on such matters as government contracts and local franchises, those men are very conscious of appearances. No matter how eminent your family, they would not readily forgive the indiscretion you just committed. The shooting of Hector MacIver is understandable. But were they to learn how you spent last night in the arms of a tan jezebel, your entire mission would fail. And I do not wish it to fail."

"And you're sure I committed an indiscretion."

The carriage slowed as the road steepened, entering a rocky canyon, its walls dotted with scraggly piñon just beginning to produce their tasty nuts.

"Quite certain, Mr. Fargo," she said in the tone of a teacher. "You emerged at dawn from the home of a notorious trollop, one of those half-breed hussies. Your garments were disheveled."

Fargo glanced once more around the interior of the phaeton, noting the rolled and pleated leather seat. In a pocket on the dashboard, just below the whip socket, he finally saw what he knew had to be close at hand—a brass spyglass. For whatever reasons, this society girl had been out on an early-morning ride. She had stopped on a rise near town, noticed something moving, and then snooped from long distance.

She thought she had something on one of the Fargos of San Francisco. Which meant she planned to use her knowledge to get something she wanted. Trouble was, she looked like a woman who already had everything she might want: an education, social position, good clothes, the wealth to afford a smooth-riding carriage with a smart-stepping team, the money to purchase a powerful telescope for a toy.

But Fargo was just along for the ride, so he waited in silence when she halted the carriage at the top of a rise and let the horses blow a bit.

Not until the wheels resumed turning did she talk again, and Fargo could swear she'd sidled over a bit as she moved the reins to her left hand and her right found its way to perch atop Fargo's thigh.

"You are a man of culture and refinement yourself, are you not?"

Fargo didn't see any reason to argue with her or the way her gloved hand felt through his pants. He extended his left arm across her shoulders, draping it on the seat top, and let her go on talking.

"Then I need not tell you how well I understand the frustrations that drove you into that sordid part of town last night."

"No," Fargo said, being careful with his words. "I suspect not."

The carriage rounded a bend in the narrowing road, rewarding them with the sight of an idyllic glen. From where they sat to the gurgling creek, knee-high grass had escaped the general summer browning to undulate in green waves with the gentle breeze. Massive cottonwoods shaded the bank of the creek. Behind the leafy trees, a sheer wall of red rock rose, its majestic sweep punctuated by a narrow cascade of water that tumbled downward, leaping from step to step in thirty-foot jumps that raised plumes of spray.

While one hand set the brake, the other found its way farther up Fargo's thigh. She nestled against his shoulder.

"There are things about Santa Fe which I like very much, Mr. Fargo, and this is one of them."

"I can see why."

She shuddered. "But, Mr. Fargo, everything else here is so horrible. I know you would understand."

"I'll try." He looked into her azure eyes and saw that she was not far from tears. "But I'm sure I'd do it better if we got out of this carriage so we could enjoy this spot a little more."

"Of course," she replied.

Fargo got out and helped her down. They settled in the thick grass, their backs against a yard-thick downed limb. A few yards before them, a clear pool caught the waterfall in splashes and gurgles. But her head was so close to Fargo's that he had no trouble hearing her.

"I shall never understand my father," she confessed. "When my mother passed away, he moved from out West from Saint Louis, but he continued to send me to boarding school and then college in Massachusetts." From the way she put r's at the ends of words that weren't supposed to have r's, and left r's off of words that should have ended that way, Fargo knew that much about her.

"When I was graduated a year ago this spring, he insisted that I come to Santa Fe."

"So you came." Sitting this way was twisting Fargo's shoulder uncomfortably, but he didn't want to disturb her, and if he shifted at all, he would.

"Only to find that I had been educated, that I knew of literature and music and art, but nothing of what women chatter about in Santa Fe. Nor are there any civilized men in that village. They're all uncouth barbarians. Even those tony swells at the Palace talk of nothing but commerce. Those who even know how to read never pick up anything besides their ledgers and waybills."

The sobs finally caught up with her as she concluded, "Mr. Fargo, I'm so lonely. There's no one to talk to here, no one who understands. You don't know what I've been through, how much I've tried, how desperate I am to live among civilized people. I'm so glad to find you." She collapsed against Fargo's chest, shuddering as she wept.

Fargo wasn't exactly traveling under false pretenses, he figured, since she'd been the one who was so damn sure she knew everything about him. Even so, it would have been stretching matters considerably for him to start quoting Shakespeare's plays or Montaigne's essays.

But it seemed foolish to start a literary discussion with a woman who so obviously wanted to be kissed. More than kissed, as Fargo discovered when he leaned down. When his lips met hers, her long slender arms responded with a viselike bear hug that pulled Fargo downward.

First his knees, and now his neck and shoulders were going to ache if he didn't shift positions. Without coming up for air while her tongue, long and slender like every other part of her, probed his mouth, Fargo responded with a grasp of his own, rolling sideways and extending himself so that he lay on his back. She had rolled right with him and now extended along his stretched form.

From the way she was moving, she planned on more than an extended kiss, especially the way she rocked sideways, using Fargo's bulk to hold her gloves as she slipped her hands free and began to caress Fargo's face and neck.

Fargo remembered some tale he'd been told. Back in King Arthur's day, some women wore chastity belts, complete with lock and key, thus preserving their virtue.

The yards and yards of cloth and fasteners that stylish modern women wore seemed to work pretty much the same way, except that a lock and key would have been simpler. Rows of tiny buttons that had to be undone in spots he could barely reach and certainly couldn't see. Successions of diminutive hooks presented the same problem as she writhed atop him in the lush grass. Fargo eventually loosened her tight weskit and flowing skirt.

But underneath, between the steel-stayed corset and the metal hoops that shaped her skirt, she seemed to be carrying more hardware than most blacksmith shops. And what in hell would such a thin woman want with a corset, anyway?

Just when he had confirmed that there was indeed a woman under the skirt and had started wondering just how to undo the corset, her ardent kissing halted. She pulled her head up and back with such sharpness that some of her hairpins slipped. Golden curls tumbled out from under her hat as it toppled off. With a sharp huff, she glared down.

"Mr. Fargo, just what do you think we're doing here?"

As smart and educated as this woman said she was, she should have known damn well what they were doing. Fargo couldn't imagine why any woman would need to ask such foolish questions, but there were some who always did.

"Making the beast with two backs," he answered slowly, watching her eyes light up at his reply.

"That's from *Othello*," she tittered. "Act One, Scene One." Her head came down again as she whispered, "I knew you were a learned man."

Fargo started kissing her again before she could utter any more praise of his erudition and culture.

To Fargo's immense pleasure, she responded with actions instead of words. Her long, slender fingers started popping buttons loose on his vest, then moved to his belt buckle. With some feverish cooperation, they shortly had each other undressed. Every now and again, she'd pause to eye Fargo's scars, but she didn't mention them. If she had, Fargo was prepared to say they were dueling scars, and leave it at that.

They ended up in pretty much the same position as they'd started. Fargo was stretched out on his back, she stretched along his front, her fingers toying with his shoulder-length hair while her small breasts, pliant but firm, traced impassioned ovals on his chiseled chest. With every rotation, she was sliding down, her taut thighs pressed against Fargo's.

They joined slowly, almost tentatively. Fargo rocked up and down on the grass as she rocked up and down his frame, pulling him in a little deeper with each thrust.

With the suddenness of a hungry cat springing for a bird, her limber legs swung around toward Fargo. She planted her knees next to his loins. She swung her torso back and perched atop Fargo's engorged staff. With a gasp, she plunged down as Fargo arched up.

Whatever she hollered, it sounded like fun, it didn't

make sense, and it echoed off the cliff for quite a while. Bouncing to get Fargo's full measure every time she came down, she sped up the tempo. Fargo, enjoying the view of her silken thighs and firm breasts, matched her stroke for stroke until he saw that she was ready. At his first pulsing surge, she drove herself downward, her shouted ecstasy again echoing from the vermilion cliff.

Judging by the short shadows, it was close to noon when they started stirring again. What with one thing and another—she had suggested a bath in the clear pool, right under the waterfall, and once they got wet, she had some other interesting notions that Fargo enjoyed—they didn't get the phaeton back to town until the shadows had begun to lengthen.

Explaining that she had certain proprieties and social obligations to observe, the smiling woman left Fargo off at his rented room. Fargo changed into more comfortable clothes and strolled over to the livery stable and saw that his Ovaro had been well tended. Then he turned toward tending himself.

The nearby aroma of beef and chili peppers was causing his stomach to start gnawing on his backbone. Fargo found a seat by the front window in a cantina, not nearly as elaborate as where he'd eaten last night. But the pungent food was just as good. Maybe even better. For sure the company was an improvement.

Leaning back in his chair while his dinner settled in him, Fargo reflected on how nice it was that women came in so many shapes, colors, and sizes, and all of them were good. It was hard to improve on a day that started with short, round Carmelita, who barely spoke English, and moved on to a lean, tall blonde who rattled on with five-dollar words while showing off her literary education. Then there were the huge helpings of fiery food, and he had a fresh beer in front of him. Even better, the evening hadn't started yet. If this held up, a summer in Santa Fe would be a season in paradise.

He was more than willing to settle back and relax a bit, but when he looked out the window, the sleepy street had become agitated. Folks were heading for the plaza.

Not exactly running, but their steps were determined and they weren't wasting any time.

Somewhat stiff-legged from the day's exercises, Fargo made his own way to the plaza.

From what he could overhear as people interspersed chatter with their huffs and puffs, an advance rider for a wagon train had just arrived, so agitated that he was shouting wildly while he came into town.

When the westbound caravans got within two hundred miles or so of Santa Fe, they always camped under a mountain whose twin pointed peaks gave it the name of Rabbit Ears. From there, they usually sent a rider on ahead, to tell folks in Santa Fe that the train was coming and to make whatever advance arrangements were necessary with the warehouses, consignment merchants, trading companies, and so forth. In early July, wagon trains that had left Missouri in April would be rolling in two or three times a week.

Santa Fe people looked forward to each arrival, because it meant they'd be able to buy everything from pins to pianos. They always crowded into the plaza when the freighters rolled into town and made the circuit before finally halting.

But they never showed this much excitement over the mere arrival of a caravan. The way folks were hustling over that way, it was more like the circus was in town or a hanging was scheduled.

"Comanches! Red devils!" The leathery horseman took off his sombrero and waved it across the crowd, then pointed east toward Apache Canyon. "I come by too late," he shouted. "All the wagons was smokin' an' the men all dead."

Fargo looked around the crowd, which was growing by the minute. Among the new arrivals was a phaeton Fargo recognized. Not far away, he spotted Lord Cavendish with a small crowd of other swells. Standing by his warehouse door, Cyrus Ashbrook was staring openmouthed at the horseman, not more than a dozen feet away.

Both the rider and the crowd settled down a bit as the man continued. "It was just over by Wagon Mound where they got hit. Them thievin', treacherous redskins snuck up an' killed all the men, looted all the wagons, an' then fired it all."

"Whose train was it?" someone shouted from the crowd.

"Don't rightly know. They were a few days ahead of us. Didn't they send in no rider?"

With that, Ashbrook's mouth fell even further open as his florid face turned floury. Fargo now knew whose train had been hit.

"That's the shits," said a stout man in front of Fargo. "Me an' Hank was plannin' a rip-roarer once he got here. And it don't sound like he'll ever get here."

"Not standin' up, anyway," commiserated his taller friend. "Don't seem fair at all. Hank's made that trip a dozen times if he done it once. If anybody could do it right, it was Hank."

Something awful clicked in Fargo's head. He leaned forward. "Excuse me, gents. But I couldn't help overhearing you. I know a wagon master named Hank, and I sure hope he's a different one from the one you're talking about."

"Was I you, I'd hope so too, mister," the stout one replied, tensing his broad shoulders. "But Hank Barclay was a damn good man to know."

A wretched taste started in the back of Fargo's mouth and spread forward. Hank Barclay. Hank Barclay *had* been a damn good man to know. Just all around a damn good man. A man to ride the river with.

A young and feisty Skye Fargo had once got in an awful jam down in Arkansas, a little misunderstanding with a sheriff who had put Fargo in jail while carpenters built a scaffold outside. Hank Barclay, even then a veteran wagon master, came through town with a load of army supplies.

Two of his teamsters got rowdy and ended up sharing a cell with Fargo two nights before the sheriff planned to stretch Fargo's neck. Barclay came down to bail out his men and stopped to talk to Fargo. After an awful commotion in the lawman's office, a bloody and bruised sheriff grudgingly let Fargo out, cussing up and down about the "high-handed way the fuckin' army thinks it can just march into town an' let criminals out of jail

41

'cause it needs hands to move its fuckin' wagons through Injun territory.''

Barclay had meant it, too. He put Fargo to work on the four-hundred-mile trip into Texas, a trip through swamps, snakes, and hostile Indians. That they'd survived at all was due to Barclay's courage and common sense. They'd parted ways, but a young Fargo had learned much from the older man. Fargo felt that he'd always owe Barclay.

Backing away, Fargo just wanted to go sit by himself for a few minutes and study what had happened and how he might repay an old obligation. There was wildfire talk of getting up some sort of posse to go punish the Comanches, and Fargo knew he'd better think for a few minutes before jumping into something like that.

Hearing sobbing sounds, Fargo looked up. The tall blond woman in the phaeton was weeping, almost convulsed in her sorrow. Fargo paused and stared, uncertain as to what he should do.

It wasn't like they didn't know each other, he thought. But no man with a lick of sense ever got between a grizzly sow and her cubs, and no man with more than a spoonful of brains ever went near a crying woman if he could avoid it. And then it struck him that they weren't really such good friends, anyway. She thought he was somebody he wasn't, and he didn't even know her name.

He felt a savage jerk on his arm that pulled him around to face a man of medium build whose three-piece suit, complete with diamond stickpin, fit him pretty well. The indignant man eyed Fargo up and down, from battered stetson to patched flannel shirt, from faded Levi's to worn boots. A sneer of contempt grew under his shiny waxed mustache.

"I catch you looking at my intended that way again, and you'll wish you'd never come to Santa Fe, cowboy.''

"Do tell." Fargo stepped back, not wanting to get drawn into a fight. He could handle the man easy enough, but he had friends with him, and there were a lot more ways to get hurt in a brawl than there were not to. "I'm sorry about that."

Fargo decided against his intended offer to shake hands,

because the man was still seething. "You got it clear that Miss Phoebe Ashbrook is spoken for? And you know that even if she weren't betrothed, she wouldn't have anything to do with a ruffian like you?"

"Just as clear as daylight," Fargo responded, wheels spinning in his head. So it was Cyrus Ashbrook who'd made his daughter come out West after finishing college in the east. "If it's all the same to you, I'll be on my way now."

By all that was right and proper, Carmelita should have been at work serving dinners right now. But when all the customers in her cantina had taken off for the excitement in the plaza, she'd joined the crowd. Now she was standing within earshot of Fargo and Phoebe's intended.

With a sizzling hiss, her brown dagger eyes fixed on Fargo. She muttered some things in rapid-fire Spanish. Fargo wasn't sure of the exact meaning of her words, but from her tone, he felt reasonably certain that Carmelita wasn't telling him how much she liked him.

This was another time when a man with any brains to speak of would be somewhere else. Before Fargo could accomplish that, though, she lunged toward him. "You got another girl, Señor Fargo?" Fargo couldn't help but glance toward the phaeton, a motion Carmelita caught. "That washed-out bitch? I'll teach that *perra blanca* not to come near my man. I'll scratch her eyes out."

Too quickly for still-stunned Fargo to grab her, she sprang toward Phoebe Ashbrook's carriage. The blond woman's intended or betrothed or whatever he was should have jumped up to protect Phoebe from Carmelita. But instead, he tried to jump Fargo from the back, hollering something about how he'd warned one hick never to look at his Phoebe ever again.

Fargo spun, rolling the man off him and sticking a boot toe into the fool's ribs. That gave him enough time to look up and see a terrified Phoebe Ashbrook shake the reins and shout at her team. The horses reared, clearing a space before them, and the carriage lurched forward, just in time to keep the short Carmelita from leaping aboard.

Fargo couldn't be sure just why Phoebe shot such a hateful look his way. It might be because that was what she thought of ill-dressed ruffians. Or it could be that she'd just figured out that her cultivated afternoon friend was in truth one of those ill-dressed ruffians. Maybe she thought he'd sent that flailing Carmelita her way.

He didn't have any more time for speculation, because Phoebe's reviving boyfriend had grabbed one of his legs and was trying to pull him down while two friends jumped him. To the surprise of all of them, Fargo cooperated and fell down. His bent knees landed right on top of the boyfriend, knocking the wind out of him.

The other two seemed interested in further rumpling their suits, so the Trailsman obliged them. He grabbed one by the vest and rolled him back, using two fingers on the other hand to poke a pair of watery eyes. When the man's head snapped back in pain, Fargo's fist clenched and slammed into his jaw.

Normally, a scuffle like this in the plaza would have drawn a crowd. But no one was interested in staying very near Phoebe's horses, bucking and snorting as she tried to dodge Carmelita. Fargo got up, resisting the temptation to kick the boyfriend for good measure. The one he'd rolled away was starting to stand up. He looked at Fargo pleadingly and turned, staggering away.

Fargo was a firm believer in doing first things first. The trouble here was deciding what came first. He ought to go gentle those frightened horses before they ran off with Phoebe or sent a flying hoof into some bystander. But if he did that, Carmelita would surely bounce up into the carriage faster than he could leave the horses and restrain her. Grabbing Carmelita first meant the horses and carriage might get away.

While the carriage spun and lurched in the dusty street, Fargo ran up next to it. He jumped inside, grabbing the reins from the astonished and speechless Phoebe. Once horses got this agitated, they were often too riled to respond to the reins, no matter how hard the bit dug into their mouths. With some clucking, pulling, and cussing Fargo persuaded the two bays to quit rearing.

Moments later, they were stepping along as if they'd

never been upset, making a circuit of the plaza as folks stepped out of their way. In a minute or so, they'd be fully settled down and they wouldn't give Phoebe any more trouble.

Not that he or Phoebe really needed any more trouble at the moment. Once the phaeton was moving smoothly and slowly, Carmelita had easily caught up to it and she was clambering aboard Phoebe's side. Both women were glaring at Fargo, one with fiery azure points and the other with blistering brown glints. But when Carmelita attacked, she went right over Phoebe's lap, straight for Fargo.

He got an arm around the flailing Carmelita and tensed, preparing to jump off and take her with him, just as soon as he could figure out how to pass the reins to Phoebe. That much was solved when she leaned their way and grabbed them, missing the turn so they went straight on down the street. Prepared to bail out, Fargo felt Carmelita jerk back, freeing his grip at the same moment as the front wheel hit a chunk of firewood in the street, and the carriage pitched.

Fargo went overboard, his quick reflexes bringing him down on his feet. He looked up to see the carriage roll smoothly on along the street, proceeding so evenly that no one would suspect that it was being pulled by two headstrong horses. Or that it carried two women who could be even more unruly.

But nothing appeared amiss as he saw it turn a corner without tipping. Fargo figured he'd best leave well enough alone. Going anywhere near that carriage now would be asking for trouble, and a man could find plenty of that without asking.

What he needed now was a drink. Or better yet, a whole bottle. He took his time walking back to the plaza. Before he got that far, he spied a traditional saloon. It wasn't adobe, and with its wooden false front and bat-wing doors, it looked out of place here.

That was how Fargo felt as he perched a foot on the rail and ordered up a bottle. It was funny how fast Santa Fe could quit being pleasant. There were two women in that carriage, and neither had much use for him at the moment. That was probably the only thing they agreed on.

Since they represented both sides of town, they could make Fargo's life fairly miserable here no matter where he went. If they started fighting now, there would be no end of scandal in Phoebe's circle, and Phoebe would blame him. She'd also find out, if she hadn't already, that the Fargo she'd been cozying up to wasn't one of the Fargos she thought worthy of her. She'd be mad about that, and Santa Fe just wasn't big enough for him to escape her rage.

Carmelita was even more difficult to figure out. Was she just warm-natured? Had she really been grateful to him for taking down Cyrus Ashbrook last night? And so Ugly John's lurking on her back door was no fault of hers? Or had it been a plan? Had she cooperated, perhaps under threat of death, to set him up?

Fargo shook his head clear and poured another shot. The only way to get rid of those worries was to move on. He wouldn't have to move far. Just about anything Santa Fe had could be found in nearby Taos.

The main reason, Fargo decided, that this ramshackle tavern so much resembled every other western saloon was that it served bad whiskey. He'd wanted smooth Kentucky bourbon. He'd had to settle for ragged corn liquor, which burned at his throat as he finished the shot and let the glass sit empty.

What burned even worse was the news about Hank Barclay. It didn't add up just right. A well-organized wagon train might get sniped at by Comanches, might even lose a man or two. But Indians didn't just charge right in. They seldom fought pitched battles because they lost too many warriors that way. Indians worked like anybody else: they wanted the maximum gain for the minimum loss.

So they'd harass a wagon train, but if nobody on the train got flustered, they were seldom a real threat. Fargo knew how Hank Barclay ran wagon trains. He'd stay in control.

A Comanche attack didn't stand to reason. And what was Hank Barclay, an experienced wagon master who doubtless had his pick of jobs last spring in Missouri, doing with a little outfit like Ashbrook's? There was another thing that didn't add right.

Fargo couldn't being his friend back to life, but he could sure as hell find out how and why Barclay had died. Barclay would have done the same for him, Fargo felt certain, and the sense of obligation the Trailsman now felt was almost overwhelming. He didn't try, didn't even want to try, to talk himself out of it.

He poured another shot and swallowed the harsh liquor. Its bitter taste, though, was not as galling as the pride he knew he was going to swallow.

He didn't like the thought of apologizing to Cyrus Ashbrook and telling him he'd changed his mind about the job. He didn't like it one bit. It was like eating shit while somebody watched and gloated.

There was only one thing worse, and that would be doing Ashbrook's job and not getting paid for it.

It was enough to drive a man to drink. Fargo felt some comfort that he was already there.

3

Doffing his wide-brimmed Stetson as he stepped inside, Fargo waited for his eyes to adjust from the brilliant sunlight of the plaza to the shadowy interior of the Ashbrook Trading Company. Although it had big glass windows in front, like all the other mercantile quarters along the row, it faced north, so the inside appeared gloomy.

He saw a room perhaps fifteen feet wide that ran back for thirty or forty feet to a wall that separated the front room from the back storeroom. A table, apparently used as a desk, sat next to the door. Along Fargo's right, a rough wooden counter extended the length of the room. Behind it were shelves that ran from the packed-dirt floor up to the low ceiling. The shelves were almost empty—a few bolts of calico and some boxes of geegaws made up all the inventory in sight.

If Hank Barclay's wagon train had come in as scheduled, those shelves would have been jammed with merchandise. The store would have been jammed with customers, all eager to trade local products like bars of silver, pokes of gold dust, big bags of rough wool, and huge Spanish jackasses that would be taken back to Missouri to be bred with broad-backed mares to produce the strongest mules the world had ever seen. And Ashbrook would profit.

Fargo glanced around again to make sure no one else was in the room. "Anybody home?" he shouted. The adobe walls swallowed his voice, which would have echoed anywhere else.

The storeroom door opened, and Fargo blinked twice to be sure he was really seeing what he thought he was seeing. He'd have preferred a pack of wildcats, but what he saw stepping through the portal was Phoebe Ashbrook.

As usual, she was dressed severely, this time in a white shirtwaist and a snuff-brown skirt. Her golden hair was pulled back in a tight bun. She looked startled for an instant, and then regained her businesslike poise.

"Why, Mr. Fargo . . ." She stared for a moment, apparently trying to decide if he was a San Francisco Fargo worthy of her manners and her attention, or some other Fargo to be dismissed as quickly as possible. "May I ask what brings you by the Ashbrook emporium?" She gathered her skirt and sat at the desk, turning to face Fargo.

"You certainly may," Fargo answered, finding a wall to slouch against.

The silence was almost tangible until she finally got around to breaking it. "Mr. Fargo, I asked you your business here, and you did not answer me."

"No, ma'am," Fargo countered. "You asked if you might ask my business. And I said you could. But you haven't got around to actually asking me my business here. And I learned a long time ago that a man stays a lot happier if he doesn't go around answering questions that he hasn't been asked."

"Very well, then," she huffed. "Mr. Fargo, what is your business here?"

"I want to talk to Cyrus Ashbrook."

"He's, uh, he's busy right at the moment." From her stammer and blush, Fargo knew that meant that Cyrus Ashbrook was indeed busy—busy sitting in the two-holer out by the alley. If the light and the reading matter were good, and the wasps that always nested in out houses were busy elsewhere today, Cyrus Ashbrook would be busy for quite a while.

Phoebe turned and began shuffling through papers in the dim light, pausing every now and again to pull one out of the sheaf and set it in a different stack. She seemed to know what she was doing.

Curious, Fargo walked back there, his steps silent on

the porous dirt floor, getting close enough to where she was a bit startled when she lifted her eyes and saw him.

"What do you find so interesting here, Mr. Fargo?" Her tone was crisper than burnt bacon.

"I don't often see women doing men's work in a business office," he replied. "I'm surprised, that's all."

"Are you saying that women are so delicate and scatterbrained that they can't handle a few papers?" She had a curious ability to be looking up at the standing Fargo and be looking down her nose at him at the same time.

"I said just what I said," he replied. "It was a surprise. I didn't say anything about what women could or couldn't do. Whatever you know, I don't think you know enough to go around putting words in my mouth."

She bristled momentarily, as if to let Fargo know that she wasn't backing down one bit, before relaxing and smiling. "I don't often come in to do men's work," she conceded. "But the regular clerk often travels on business, so I have become accustomed to coming in and doing what must be done. There are so many more pleasant ways to spend a day, though."

Fargo saw what was likely a wink, but in this shadowy area, he wasn't positive. He nodded, and she continued. "I believe you have met the man who normally handles the paperwork here, Mr. William Fletcher."

That name didn't ring any bells, so Fargo shook his head.

"Oh, that's right," she explained. "You were never formally introduced. But I know you met him yesterday evening." She paused and noticed that Fargo still had no idea who William Fletcher might be. "Meeting you last night was the reason that he became so indisposed that he could not come into work today. Mr. Fletcher is the man who says he is my fiancé."

Trying to forget all the things that had happened last evening was the main reason Fargo had been so fond of corn liquor last night.

"Well," he finally answered, wishing fervently that Cyrus Ashbrook would hurry back from his morning chores, "I surely do hope that you didn't have any more trouble with your horses last night."

"Not at all, Mr. Fargo. I should have thanked you for your bravery, but it sometimes seem that every time one attempts to solve a difficulty, the solution brings even greater difficulties."

Fargo decided that the women of Santa Fe certainly had their talents, but communication wasn't on the list. Carmelita might talk basic English, but you could never be sure what she was up to. Phoebe Ashbrook spoke perfect English, but spun her words in webs and circles: webs to trap men, and circles to confuse them.

Fargo stretched his husky frame, noticed that yesterday's aches had acquired some relatives, and changed the subject.

"So you had to come in to shuffle the papers, instead of going for a carriage ride into the hills."

She sighed and blushed a bit. She was so pale that even in this dim light, her flush was obvious.

"That awful tragedy, losing a whole wagon train to the Indians."

She choked, then regained her composure. "That's dreadful, of course, but life goes on, Mr. Fargo. There was insurance, and we have to send notices to our insurers. Most of our financial losses will eventually be repaid, but I understand that insurance companies are generally in no hurry to settle matters. I hope I can prepare everything in time to meet this week's post at noon."

Fargo realized she did need to hurry. The mail stage ran only once a week. The sooner she got those papers sent off, the sooner her father would get some kind of settlement. And if Ashbrook had been losing wagons as regularly as he said he had been, the man might never get insurance again, which could pretty well put him out of business.

"I'll get out of your way, then," Fargo said, "I'll just watch the fountain in the plaza until your father returns. Just holler out the door or send him over to see me."

"Oh, no, Mr. Fargo. You're quite welcome here. I do wish Billy were here, though. He's so good with all this

51

paperwork. Father was fortunate to find someone like Billy."

"He does seem to think a lot of you," Fargo commented, ready to spin on his boot and head for the plaza.

"More than he ought," she added, speaking softly to Fargo's retreating back. "Billy tells everyone we are engaged, although I have yet to give formal consent to his continuing proposals. He is terribly jealous, but can be so thoughtful at times. No matter what I ask, or even hint about, he is always so willing to perform. Sometimes his eagerness almost frightens me."

Her voice caught, and Fargo turned back at the doorway to see the tall woman stretching in her chair, not at all in a hurry about the important papers that sat behind her as she turned, a perplexed expression on her face. "Mr. Fargo, I believe my father can see you now. Just step through here. His office is on your right."

With its small west window and whitewashed walls, Ashbrook's private office was much better lit than the trade room up front. The portly man rose from his battered rolltop desk and greeted Fargo so enthusiastically that all three of his chins were going in different directions. He pumped Fargo's hand, offering a cigar and drink, both of which Fargo declined with thanks. No sense adding to last night's ill effects.

"Mr. Fargo, I'm so glad you've come by." Ashbrook wetted the cigar, a short, stubby brand that sold three for a nickel anywhere in civilization and fetched a full dime in Santa Fe. He struck a lucifer match on the thick adobe interior wall and lit the cigar. "I've had people looking all over town for you."

Fargo lifted his eyebrows as a reply. Ashbrook motioned to a straight-backed wooden chair, then slumped his plump body into his own comfortable seat. Fargo took the hint, to sit and listen as Ashbrook's voice fell to a hoarse whisper.

"It's awful, despicable, losing that wagon train. It was our big hope to come out with a profit on this season. Our agents in Missouri recruited the best man they could find to run that train, the very goddamn best. Those wagons were going to get through. And then to hear what we all heard last night. Jesus."

"I knew Hank Barclay."

Ashbrook shook his head and lifted it. "Mr. Fargo, what happened to Hank Barclay was awful. It shouldn't happen to any man, especially a man like him. I never met him face to face, but if he was half as good as folks said he was, then he was a man to make book on. And there were two dozen more men on that train, and they're all dead." The chubby man sighed and his complexion grew ashen. "But sometimes I think the living might envy the dead."

Fargo had never felt any particular jealousy for corpses, so he pressed Ashbrook.

"The dead go to whatever they go to. We who remain have to go on living. And why? For years I've tried to build up a trade, and I'm going to lose it all. Even if I collect the insurance they gouged me for, it won't arrive in time to do me any good. And I probably won't collect. You know how insurance companies are. They'll find some goddamn little legalistic thing in the contract that says they don't have to pay on an Indian raid unless I give them two weeks' advance notice of the raid."

Ashbrook settled back into his chair and chewed thoughtfully on his cigar, which had gone out. "But this is all I have. We made money for several years, good money, but this past year . . ."

His voice trailed off. He shook his head and picked up some steam. "I'm losing wagons and I'm losing men and I'm losing goods. Somebody is sure trying to put me out of business, me and a couple other small freighters and traders."

"You're sure of that?" Fargo asked.

"It doesn't add up much of any other way," Ashbrook explained. "I know you think I'm an idiot, Mr. Fargo, but I hope you came this morning because you've reconsidered on what you said the other night. I know I have."

"I'm busy trying to reconsider on what I did last night," Fargo said, trying to put a light tone on his words. "And now I wish things had turned out different the night before."

Some animation crept into Ashbrook's pudgy face and he chuckled. "Ah, shit, I had too much to drink. It don't take much drinking any more for me to make a goddamn fool out of myself. Ever since Martha died, I get a couple beers in me, and I act like a billy goat, even when I'm supposed to be talking business. I had it coming, Mr. Fargo. You certainly don't owe me any apologies."

Fargo wasn't about to pay what he didn't owe, so he shifted the conversation. "I came by today to talk business."

Ashbrook nodded. "I hoped so. But I don't think there'll be much to discuss."

Fargo's spirits fell. He'd go after whoever got Hank Barclay, be it Comanche, Comanchero, Texican, Mexican, Apache, or plain old American thief. But he sure wanted to be paid for his trouble, and if that meant kissing Cyrus Ashbrook's ass for a few minutes, Fargo would even do that. But now what was Ashbrook up to?

With a glum grunt, the Trailsman acknowledged Ashbrook's statement.

The merchant looked directly at Fargo, coughed and hemmed for a moment, and got around to saying what he had to say. "Mr. Fargo, I can't speak for the other men who were with us when we last talked. But I can speak for myself. I want to hire you to find and bring to justice whoever it is that struck our wagon train."

Ashbrook coughed again and did not bring his eyes back up. A mumble crept into his gravelly voice. "You might not be the only man on earth who can do that job, Mr. Fargo. But the only other one I can think of is tied up in Albuquerque with the army. I need you. You can write your own ticket, do whatever you must do to get the job done. I'll back you as far as I can, and I'll pay you so much as I can."

"That's pretty much what you offered the other night," Fargo replied, savoring the moment. He'd expected to have to crawl to Ashbrook, and now Ashbrook was doing all the bowing and scraping. "And then your little committee seemed to spout fool ideas. I was supposed to report regular, like there was a telegraph out there or something, like I want to work for people that trust me

54

so goddamn much that they want to be looking over my shoulder all the time."

Fargo recollected some of the other galling parts of their previous meeting before continuing.

"And you all had your own ideas of where I was supposed to look first. Well, no, first you said I ought to scout the whole damn trail, as far as it took. Then each of you came up with a pet thief, Comanche or whatever. Then I hear it has to be Russell, Majors, and Waddell, which makes about as much sense as blaming the man in the moon. I was supposed to start on one of those, I guess.

"But how in jumping hell was I supposed to know where to start when you all said that I couldn't check your records, because those were confidential business matters that you couldn't trust outsiders around? And I wasn't supposed to talk to any of your help, neither, because that might worry them for no good reason or scare them so they might up and quit and go work for somebody else. And I was supposed to behave like a gentlemen at all times while in your employ, because you didn't want any of your snooty associates thinking that you'd consort with a ruffian . . ."

"Enough, enough," Ashbrook thundered. "You do it your way, Fargo. It's your job and you're the expert. Whatever you want from me, it's yours." He reached for a pigeonhole as he continued, chuckling. "Except perhaps Phoebe, of course." Ashbrook didn't see Fargo's broad and wicked grin, because he was staring at a piece of paper before handing it to Fargo. "Here's your retainer, Fargo."

Fargo looked down at the sheet and whistled. It was a bank draft for two thousand dollars.

"I don't know how much more there will be to pay you with, Fargo. But let me put it this way. I expect the best that you can do. Which means you have every right to expect the best that I can do."

"That's fair," Fargo replied as he stood up. "I'll earn it."

Ashbrook rose, beaming and nodding.

They hadn't finished shaking hands when they heard

some sort of ruckus on the other side of the wall. The sounds were muffled, but hearing them at all from where they stood meant that things had to be pretty noisy in the outer room. Fargo spun around, almost pulling Ashbrook with him, jerked the office door open, and turned toward the insubstantial door that led to the dark front room.

Knowing that a man coming through a doorway presented an easy target, and not knowing just what was going on out there, Fargo placed a thoughtful hand on his Colt and stopped to eavesdrop.

"If I've told you once, I've told you a thousand times, William, that Mr. Fargo is consulting my father on business and they're not to be disturbed."

"And, honey, I've told you and told you and told you—and you never listen, you never listen to anything I tell you—that this Mr. Fargo is not who you think he is. He's not from San Francisco. He is not related in any way to William Fargo of Wells Fargo. He is not a gentleman. He is a ruffian, a scoundrel, a no-account drifter."

"Whoever he is, he is with my father, and you are not to disturb them."

Fargo sure heard the finality in her voice, but poor Billy Fletcher must have had something wrong with his ears.

"And I've got to get in there and warn your father before this Fargo character deceives him, the way he pulled the wool over everyone's eyes. But I now know who he really is, and I can prove it."

Cyrus Ashbrook was by now standing right next to Fargo, breathing heavy and looking fretful. "Fargo, you got any idea what he's talking about?" he whispered.

"If I did, do you think I'd tell you?" Fargo softly chortled in reply, putting his finger to his lips. They again leaned forward to cock their ears to the door's thin panels.

Just as they bent forward, Billy Fletcher gave up on arguing with Phoebe and jerked the door open. A flabbergasted Cyrus Ashbrook rolled through and down, landing face-first on the packed-dirt floor, his arms spread helplessly. Fargo caught himself in time to avoid hitting the floor; he managed to stick one booted foot out in front of his body and land in a crouch.

That left him in a perfect position to receive a robust kick to his rib cage that knocked the wind out of his chest. Momentarily too stunned to think, Fargo relied on his reflexes and lashed out with his arm, trying to grab the swift shiny leather boot and pull it's owner down.

Fargo's flailing thrust wasn't fast enough and he lost his precarious balance, sprawling forward. As he started to get his feet under him, a boot landed on his ass and rammed him back to the floor. Rolling over onto his back and pulling his knees up to protect his groin, Fargo wormed to the wall before turning to get a good look at his assailant.

From Fargo's low vantage, medium-sized Billy Fletcher loomed like a rising colossus. What most impressed Fargo, though, was the shiny nickel-plated derringer in Fletcher's right hand. Even in this dim, shadowy room, its plating glittered in contrast with the deep ominous darkness of its .42-caliber barrel.

Before Fargo could say anything, Fletcher started talking in a reedy tenor, the words tumbling one after the other.

"You're right, cowboy. I don't fight fair. I kicked your ass when you were down, and I'll kick it again if I feel like it. You make one move toward that big Colt on your hip, and I'll plaster such brains as you might have against that wall. I've taken all I'm ever going to take from you."

"You won't hear me argue with that," Fargo answered levelly, meeting Fletcher's gray-wolf eyes with his own icy blue stare.

"Now, Mr. Fargo, will you be so kind as to tell everyone here just who you really are and why you're really in Santa Fe?"

"You already know my name is Fargo, but I can repeat it if it makes you feel better. Fargo. F-A-R-G-O. Got that? I can go a little slower if you didn't catch it all."

Fletcher clenched his teeth and pursed his lips as the irritation rose in a flush, crossing his shiny waxed mustache and then pushing his eyes into a tighter squint. His derringer began to quiver, ever so slightly, providing more evidence that the man's nerves were tight and getting tighter by the moment.

"Don't play games with me, Fargo. Just tell the truth. You've been pretending you're somebody important, and you're not. You're just some tumbleweed half-breed gunslick that calls himself Skye Fargo, aren't you?"

"Quarter-breed, if it's all the same to you." Moving as slowly, softly, and deliberately as he spoke, Fargo sat upright. With a better view of the room, he saw Phoebe in her chair, her eyes full of pinpoint contempt as she glared in their direction. Cyrus had managed to get on his feet and shuffle over to stand next to Phoebe. Fargo had seen bronze statues in parks that looked more likely to move than Cyrus did.

"Just stay still, cowboy." The quiver had worked its way up to Fletcher's vocal cords. He glanced down at his fluttering pistol before resuming his scowl at Fargo. "Now answer another question for me, Fargo." Fletcher took a couple of deep breaths, but they didn't settle him down. His voice shook as he continued. "What were you and my Phoebe doing yesterday? Why were you looking at her last night?"

"Same reason I'm looking at her now." Fargo grinned. "Same reason I turn my head whenever I catch sight of a handsome woman. It's the way I'm built. It's the way most men are built, except for them dudes that like boys instead of girls. If you're one of them, I don't quite know how I might explain it all to you." Back behind Fletcher, Phoebe and Cyrus were finally showing signs of life as they suppressed their laughter.

"You son of a bitch. You're going to answer me. What were you and Phoebe doing yesterday?"

"I don't see it as anybody's business just how I might spend time with a lady." Fargo stretched some, shrugging shoulders while pulling his knees up just a bit. He wiggled his feet in his boots, the way cats wiggle their tails before pouncing.

"It is my business. We're engaged to be married."

Phoebe audibly bristled at those words while Fargo got

in his reply. "Why don't you take that up with her, then? Or could it be that you're the one that's pretending to be something he's not?"

The rustling of Phoebe's skirt sounded loud enough to echo in the stillness, and Fletcher's nerves were now wound up tight as fiddlestrings, and they got tighter as Fargo continued. "Seems to me that if you're betrothed to Miss Ashbrook, then you ought to be able to ask her about it. Why don't you? It couldn't be all that hard, even for somebody no smarter than you are, since she's right behind you."

Billy Fletcher twitched his head to see if Phoebe was indeed right behind him. Instantly rolling forward to transfer his weight to the balls of his feet, Fargo sprang toward Fletcher, arms outstretched as his head rammed Fletcher's vest buttons.

The outraged clerk toppled backward, his pinned arms wriggling as he stumbled. Somehow he kept his feet under him, even when Fargo brought his head up, hard against Fletcher's chin. It was a toss-up as to which now hurt worse, Fargo's head or Fletcher's jaw.

Ignoring the way the jolt amplified his hangover, Fargo clasped his big hands behind Fletcher's back, hoping a bear hug would suppress the man's windmill flailing with that damned derringer.

Although Fletcher's elbows were locked tight against his sides, he could still move his hands enough to bring the gun around. No telling where a shot might go, the way Fletcher was twitching and twisting. Most likely into the dirt floor or the dirt wall. Maybe into Fletcher's employer or fiancé, though, and Fargo figured they probably weren't real eager to be targets. Fargo sure as hell had better things to do.

But as long as Fargo kept trying to squeeze Fletcher, there wasn't any way to grab the gun, and there was every chance that the red-faced idiot might pull the trigger.

As they waltzed around and around, Fargo caught glimpses of Cyrus Ashbrook, who had the frustrated look of a man who'd like to help but didn't know how and was scared to try. For her part, Phoebe looked more disgusted than if she'd found a turd floating in her wineglass. Neither one showed sense enough to get out of a room where a gun could go off in any direction at any time.

Fargo relaxed his pressure, drawing back until each hand had a chunk of Fletcher's pin-striped vest. Hopping on his left leg, Fargo brought up his right until he could plant his boot sole on the clerk's midriff. At the same instant that he released his grip on the vest, Fargo extended his powerful leg.

Billy Fletcher had so far exhibited little of a cat's agility, but the man resembled a cat in one respect: no matter how much he got thrown around, he stayed on his feet . . . even when he was teetering backward, right through the front door he had left open.

Fargo came right after him, ready to draw his Colt once they were outside, but hoping he wouldn't have to. He didn't. Fletcher, still struggling for balance, waved the derringer between them. Fargo snatched the clerk's soft hand with crushing force and Fletcher lost his grip. The gun dropped into the street.

Putting all he had into a twist of his torso and shoulder, Fargo flung out his arm and released his grip, as if he were throwing a rock. Billy Fletcher spun in a couple of clumsy pirouettes.

Likely he would have kept his feet under him this time, too, but for a complication. There was a horse trough that he backed into. Its long edge cracked him on the back of his knees. His feet finally failed him, flying up as he folded, landing butt-first in the narrow trough.

He'd come down so hard that he was jammed in there, amid the moss and several thousand buzzing insects, annoyed by the disruption. On Fargo's side, Fletcher's feet were kicking helplessly into the air. He had landed so that his arms were pinned behind him so tightly that he couldn't bend far enough forward to pull them free. On the far side of the trough, just some twisting shoulders and a sputtering head showed above the murky water. Whenever he wasn't spouting dirty water, he was sputtering some awful things about Fargo's ancestors.

It was close to the noon hour, when Santa Fe indulged in its daily three-hour siesta and nothing moved except the flies, so Fargo was mildly surprised to notice a cheerful spectator coming his way, and he had no trouble recognizing the hulking man.

"Anything I can do to help you out here, Fargo?" Ugly Jack asked through such gaping, chipped yellow teeth as his mouth held. "I figure I owes you one."

As Fargo had surmised, Ugly Jack had his faults, but he was as loyal as a collie. When the man figured you and he were on the same side, he'd do whatever he could for you. And Ugly Jack now seemed to understand that what was done was done, that there wasn't any reason to bear a grudge against Fargo.

"Thanks for the offer, ugh, er, Jack," Fargo responded, offering a handshake that was accepted. "But I reckon it's all under control." The more the helpless Billy Fletcher kicked and writhed, the farther his folded body slid toward Fargo and Jack, and the higher the water rose around his neck. He'd quieted down considerable after realizing his predicament.

"You was right, Fargo, that they might be hirin' here," Jack said. "They ain't got a lot of work right now, though. Mr. Ashbrook told me to just come in in the afternoons. Today he wants me to shovel out some of the stable."

"Glad to hear it, Jack." Fargo saw that Phoebe and Cyrus had finally summoned up the courage and curiosity to come to the door. Cyrus still looked flustered, but he did smile when he saw Billy's boots waving over the horse trough. Getting Phoebe to smile, the way her shoulders were set and her eyes glared, would probably take a hammer and chisel.

"Look, Jack," Fargo announced, "I'm working for Ashbrook now, too. And if it's okay with him, I've got a little chore for you."

Ashbrook nodded, so Fargo continued. "He and I have some more talking to do this afternoon, and then I'm leaving town first thing in the morning. As long as I'm in town, I don't want to be bothered by that mess over there in the horse trough. You think you could fish him out, and then make sure he stays out of my way?"

Jack nodded. "Any notions as to what I oughtta do with him till you get going?"

"Entirely up to you, Jack. Just make goddamn sure his path don't cross mine."

Jack brightened as an idea occurred to him. Stepping over to the other side of the horse trough, he clasped his calloused hands under Fletcher's clamped jaw and pulled the clerk upward, then backward.

Fletcher struggled and cussed a little, once his feet hit the ground, but by then Ugly Jack had enough of a hammerlock on him to teach the loudmouthed clerk a few manners. The etiquette lesson continued as a grinning Ugly Jack frog-marched the dripping and reluctant clerk down the street.

As they lumbered away, Jack turned to shout that they'd be by in the morning, ready for work, and then gave Billy's arm another twist. Cyrus Ashbrook's smile fell when Phoebe icily informed him that, on account of the morning's disruptions, the insurance papers weren't done in time for the noon stage, so it would be next week before anything got sent to Saint Louis. When she turned to Fargo, she had the expression of a woman who'd just found a worm in an apple, but she didn't say anything.

So Cyrus and Fargo left her standing there and went back to the office.

"Like I told you, Cyrus," Fargo said as they returned to their chairs, "I don't rightly know where to start. To keep from wasting a lot of time once I'm out along the trail, I've got to ask a lot of questions, and some of them will likely sound mighty dumb."

On the wall to the left of the desk was a yard-long fly-splattered map of the southwestern territories of the United States, one put together by the Army Corps of Topological Engineers. Fargo stepped over to look at it, and paused to marvel.

Just about every line engraved on it was inaccurate in some respect or another. The Rio Grande started too far north and the Arkansas too far south. All sorts of rivers were shown crossing the Great Plains, and there weren't really rivers in those spots, or any steady water of any kind within a hundred miles. No wonder, Fargo thought, that folks so often managed to get themselves lost when they trusted maps.

Ashbrook rose to stand next to him, his head barely reaching Fargo's shoulders. "Not much of a map, is it?" he said.

"It's kind of pretty, all those wiggly lines. Lot of fine drawing there," Fargo noted.

"As long as we're looking at it, I'll explain our problems," Ashbrook said. "For the first three years, everything went well enough. We'd lose a wagonload once in a while to a bad river crossing, and every now and again, some fool would ride off from the train by himself, and no doubt ended up entertaining the Comanches for two or three days while they staked him out and built a slow fire atop his belly. But those are the usual risks."

"When did the unusual risks start up?" Fargo asked.

"Last summer, I reckon." Ashbrook shrugged. "Mr. Lo was rambunctious, and besides that, the plains were so dry that even the jackrabbits carried canteens and compasses. So our train took the Mountain Branch. They got over Raton without losing anything more than a mule or two."

Ashbrook's manicured but tobacco-stained index finger traced the route southward. "Right about there, a day or so out of Cimarron, some bandits or mayhaps Indians hit the train at night. Fortunately, I guess, our crew was mostly Missouri white-trash pukes, and to hear them tell it, they fought like cornered badgers. Even so, we lost five wagons out of fifty."

"I don't recall that anybody else had too much trouble on the trail last year," Fargo mused.

"If they did, they kept quiet about it," Ashbrook agreed. "But that kind of thing happens to everybody sometimes. Those risks are why these damned cigars cost so much more in Santa Fe than in Saint Louis."

Fargo nodded, noting that the blue smoke at least kept the flies away. "So what makes you think you're being picked on?"

"Our return train that fall was more of a drive than a wagon trip, because we were herding about four hundred head of mules and jackasses. Every goddamn one of 'em got stampeded and disappeared when they were two days out of Fort Union. It looked like a Comanche job, except . . ."

"Except," Fargo finished, "that the Comanche are known as the Horse People, and they're too goddamn proud to steal mules or donkeys."

"Precisely," Ashbrook said. "But somebody sure ended up with a lot of our animals. The wagon men figured it wasn't safe to stay around and investigate, so they just kept moving. At least the wool and the bullion got to Missouri."

"Anything else?" Fargo asked.

Ashbrook reached into his vest for a new cigar and caught Fargo's nod. The way the room was filling up with smoke, Fargo figured he might as well have his own cigar, if only for self-defense. The portly merchant pulled out two, and Fargo stooped to get his lit off Ashbrook's before the merchant continued explaining his company's run of bad luck.

"Go back to when the caravan got here last fall. We had the usual big trading days, but most of the goods went to my warehouse. When all the caravans hit town at about the same time, you can't get as good a price for your goods as you can the next March or thereabouts, when you might be the only store in town with a bolt of calico or a keg of nails. Anyway, winter was just settling in good, must have been toward the middle of November, and my warehouse got raided."

"The one right out this door?" Fargo asked. "Right here in the middle of town?"

"That very one," Ashbrook agreed. "One night a bunch of men just drove in aboard some wagons and started rolling out my merchandise."

"The local law do anything about it?" Fargo inquired, half glad that his cigar had already gone out. Santa Fe had good beer and good food, but it wasn't the place for a man who liked fine whiskey or quality cigars. He was withholding judgment on the women.

Ashbrook laughed without humor. "The police here are as worthless as teats on a boar, if you want my opinion. They came down and looked at the busted-open back door and the footprints and wagon tracks and they said that sure enough, I'd been robbed."

"And then there was Hank Barclay's train," Fargo said, fighting off the sick feeling he got whenever he had to think about it.

"They were on the Cimarron Cut-off," Ashbrook said, his voice betraying his worry and anger. He moved his finger down on the map. "As best I know, they'd crossed the Canadian, but they hadn't reached Wagon Mound when they got hit. And that's a total loss. All the way around, it's a loss."

Fargo stretched. He felt imprisoned in this tiny room, choked by its smoke and confined by the walls that seemed to get closer by the dragging minute. "Cyrus, I can see why you think somebody's trying to put you out of business. You've caught more trouble in one year than most outfits get in five or ten, and you're right, it can't be just some quirk of fate."

Ashbrook shuffled to his chair and sat down wearily. "Whatever it is, Fargo, I'm counting on you to stop it."

4

The morning dew was still bright and glistening on the weathered corral posts at the livery stable when Fargo consoled his big Ovaro about having company on this trip. Fargo wasn't all that happy about bringing an extra along, either.

But this was one of those trips that could last anywhere from a week to three months. Fargo was as talented as any white man at living off the land, hunting and fishing and even grubbing roots when necessary. This trip, though, could take them into a vast territory so barren that no one could find a living on its windswept, baked terrain, so flat and featureless that early travelers had to drive wooden stakes into the ground just so they'd have landmarks. As nearly as anybody could figure, the only thing the Staked Plains were good for was to hold the rest of the world together.

It only made sense to be more than prepared if the trail of Hank Barclay's killers led them into the Staked Plains of eastern New Mexico and the Texas Panhandle. Which meant more gear than usual. Which meant a way to carry the extra gear. Which meant a goddamn pack mule.

Mules had their virtues. They could do more work on less grain that a similar-sized horse. Their smaller, harder hooves gave them fewer problems crossing rough ground. They got by on less water. Fargo knew all this. That's why he had decided on taking a mule, and the hostler up at the stable office had told Fargo that fifteen dollars would get him his pick of the mules in back.

This particular brute looked the biggest, sleekest, and healthiest of the fifty or so that were lounging around the corral not long after greeting the sunrise with a jarring cacophony of braying and whistling. Likely it was the most contrary, too, but Fargo figured he was mean and persistent enough to manage.

Both mules and donkeys, Fargo knew, had long memories. You could pretty well tell how a previous owner had abused an animal, just by what the critter shied from. This mule's nightmares must have featured a short chunk of chain. Fargo had just gone through the lengthy ritual of cinching up the packsaddle, when he spied a few rusted links of old harness chain, packed down in the dirt. Some animals had no better sense than to eat such things and give themselves a bellyache. Fargo bent down and grabbed the potential hazard.

Rusted chains don't jingle all that much, but the tinkling was enough to convince the suspicious and wary mule that Fargo intended to beat it within an inch of its life. The beast decided to strike first.

Four sharp hooves, each shod with fresh steel, started flying in at least a dozen directions. Caught by surprise, Fargo took a stunning kick to the core of his chest. It was a blow that ought to have knocked him down, but he didn't dare go down where he could get stomped by the bucking, kicking mule.

Doubled over and panting, he shuffled his boots backward, hoping to get out of range before he collapsed. Another slicing hoof hammered Fargo's kneecap, rolling his torso back and opening him to a thigh-bruising wallop that just missed his balls.

Fargo rolled back another couple yards, and then the pain took over. Gritting his teeth and squinting, he stared at the exploding mule and saw that the corral post would break before the strong rawhide tie rope would. Out of the mule's reach, Fargo felt as safe as he was likely to get for a while, and he lay back in the dust, pulling in huge gasps of cool morning air.

Both he and the mule had pretty much returned to normal when Fargo, still on his back trying to find shapes in the clouds to take his mind off the agonizing throbs that still came up from his legs and rib cage, heard a carriage rolling behind him. Sitting up gingerly, he slowly turned his head to recognize the man Santa Fe knew as Lord Cavendish, driving a jaunty surrey drawn by a handsome pair of dapple-gray German coach horses.

"Good morning, my good man," Cavendish called out. "This promises to be a capital day, does it not?"

Fargo resisted the temptation to say something like "Why, Perk Doyle, you old son of a bitch, how've you been?"

Instead, he replied with a simple, grunted "Does look that way, your Excellency." But it was a bit galling to be sitting in the dust and horse turds, hurting like a bad tooth, all on account of trying to do something useful, when this gadfly parasite con man was so obviously enjoying life.

After a couple more pleasantries, Lord Cavendish was ready to move on when Fargo recalled that there was one chore that really ought to be done before leaving Santa Fe. Knowing that his Excellency wasn't about to step out of the surrey where there was a chance of getting shit on his boots, Fargo asked the gambler to wait while he persuaded his body to stand and walk over to the carriage.

"You seem to be doing all right, Doyle."

"Fargo, I know you saved me inside the Palace Club, and I'm as grateful as a man can get, but for God's sake, please don't call me Doyle. It would ruin everything if word got out."

Fargo smiled. "I know that." In the ensuing silence, he watched placidly as twinges of anxiety appeared on Doyle's lean face.

"Okay, Fargo, what is it that you want?" Doyle was starting to sweat and fidget, looking nervously around, as if some of the magpies over in the trees might overhear whatever they were saying and spread the truth about Lord Cavendish all over New Mexico Territory.

"I just need a favor while I'm out of town." Fargo spoke deliberately, enjoying the way Doyle tried not to look edgy when he was really getting more wound up by the minute.

"Whatever I can do, I will do." The gambler's voice betrayed a smoothness that came from effort.

"Shouldn't be hard," Fargo replied. Without going into detail as to his reasons, he asked the pretender to keep his eyes and ears open for anything concerning the Ashbrook Trading Company or any of the Ashbrooks. Fargo knew he'd need some independent source of information about what went on in Santa Fe while he was gone, and the threat of exposure would probably keep Perk Doyle reasonably close to the truth.

"Be glad to," Doyle answered, sounding as though he meant it. "Won't bother me one bit to keep an eye or two on that Phoebe Ashbrook." He shook the reins and clucked. As the carriage bounced around the stable yard and toward the street, Fargo fetched the panniers and checked to make sure nothing inside them rattled like chain.

He'd spent the early part of last night rounding up supplies and packing them into the panniers. With an improvised balance beam, he'd shuffled stuff around until there wasn't more than a bean's worth of difference in weight between the twin canvas bags.

The mule wasn't exactly grateful to Fargo for all that work in preparing a balanced load, but it didn't kick at all and only tried to bite twice as the panniers went aboard, followed by Fargo's bedroll in the center of the pack rig.

If is wasn't one thing this morning, it was another. Just after Fargo got a diamond hitch slung and tied over the bedroll, a bowlegged man with a good start on a pot belly ambled up along the fence, stopping up in front of the mule. Shorter than Fargo, he was sort of low-browed and stoop-shouldered, with a tobacco-brown soup-strainer mustache.

Nothing was too distinguished about the fellow, except for a seven-pointed silver star pinned to his leather vest and the twin revolvers he wore in low holsters.

"You'd be Skye Fargo." The deputy marshal tended to clip his words, a distinction in a land where most folks took their time whenever they had anything to say.

"Been called worse," Fargo answered as calmly as he

could. He stepped around to join the man in front of the hammerheaded mule.

The deputy drew up a tight smile. "You ain't gonna much like this, Fargo, but I'm gonna have to take you in." He didn't look at all displeased about the notion, and he had a ready hand on one of the Colts, just in case Fargo might be inclined to dispute the matter.

"You just might be the man to do that," Fargo conceded. "But I'm curious. Think you could tell me who you are and just why I ought to come with you? Or do I have to guess on just how fast you can pull out that Colt?"

The deputy's brown eyes squinted. "This here star oughtta tell you all you need to know. But since you're so intent on actin' stupid this morning, I'll educate you some. I'm Virgil Clanborne, the deputy town marshal. And you killed a man the other night in our jurisdiction."

"Man's innocent till proven guilty," Fargo said, "and besides that, it was self-defense, pure and simple."

"That's as may be," Clanborne answered, his words getting even more clipped and rapid, to where he was almost hissing them out. "But that's for the judge and jury to decide when court takes up. Which'll be in a month or two. And you'll just have to wait around for it."

Fargo could think of about a thousand places he'd rather be than crammed inside a sweltering cell, getting fed slop for two months while an already cold trail grew colder. That is, if he ever got out to follow that trail. As crooked as politics could get around here, the dead rancher's kinfolk might have enough pull to frame and hang Fargo.

He studied on his options. Clanborne was as tough and fast as a frontier lawman had to be. Swinging at him would work only if the blow came so swift and fast that the man would be knocked out instantly. There was never a guarantee of that, and if Clanborne was conscious at all after a punch, bullets would be flying Fargo's way. Trying to draw on him didn't make any more sense.

Fargo looked over into the corral, then glanced at the mule, who stood less than a yard away, staring right at them as if it were interested in their conversation. The Trailsman's eyes continued to twitch, and he suddenly looked mighty restless to Deputy Clanborne. Fargo's shoulders twitched and he made and unmade fists, although he was careful to keep his hands up, away from his own revolver.

"You gonna come along peaceably, Fargo?"

Fargo shrugged and looked unpredictable. With smooth and practiced motion, Clanborne drew a revolver with his left hand. "Just don't try anything funny, Fargo." He paused with a pensive look for a moment or two. "Just to make sure you don't, I think I'll cuff you for your walk down to the calaboose. You just turn some to face the fence and get your hands behind you."

Fargo sighed and turned. He leaned toward the fence, so relaxed that his knees sagged a little. He grabbed the top rail with his right hand and stuck the left behind him for Clanborne's benefit. A relieved Clanborne reached around behind himself with his right hand, digging into a rear pocket of his baggy trousers to bring up a pair of shiny, jingling handcuffs.

That is, he tried to bring them up. Fargo didn't really see what happened next, because he sprang upward and vaulted over the corral fence, landing hard and in a heap. Once he got himself sorted out and standing up, he looked back where he'd been.

There was a loud and furious flurry of mule. Mule teeth under pulled-back ears, trying to bite a chunk out of the chain-wielding tormentor. Muscular mule legs spraying out in a brutal circle of mayhem. Sharp mule hooves slashing to ensure that the creature with the chain wouldn't have a chance to abuse any innocent muleflesh.

Pinned between the mule and the fence, Clanborne was no longer any threat to either Fargo or the mule. He was still on his feet, even after one arm had been bitten and the other kicked to numbness. Before Fargo got to the open fence, the mule delivered a swift hoofstroke to Clanborne's midsection, doubling the man over. The next big kick caught the lawman's head, and he began to crumple.

Fargo knelt and stuck his arms through the opening

beneath the bottom rail. All he could grab was Clanborne's arm, but that was enough to pull the lawman inside the fence, although Fargo couldn't get the job done in time to keep Clanborne's legs from getting stomped and kicked a few more times.

The Trailsman satisfied himself that Clanborne would come around in a while. None of the cuts or bites looked all that serious, and the man's pulse and shallow breathing seemed regular enough. And the rambunctious, chain-hating mule settled down considerable after seeing Clanborne knocked out in the dirt, so Fargo didn't have a bit more trouble getting out of Santa Fe that summer morning.

Nor did he run into trouble for the next few days. He did run across several Santa Fe–bound caravans, the bullwhackers and muledrivers all as eager to get drunk and laid as the merchants were to get their wares to market. All were pleased enough to chat with Fargo and to coffee him if it was mealtime, and they'd all heard about what was already being called the Barclay Massacre.

But even the veteran trail scouts he encountered, men whose considerable skills were like Fargo's, had little more than conjecture as to what might have happened to Hank Barclay's wagon train back there between Wagon Mound and the crossing of the Canadian.

If Fargo had been collecting heat, dust, and flies, this trip would have been something to brag on. As it was, he was just getting tired and bored late one afternoon when he reined up the Ovaro and the trailing mule on a rise in the rolling desolation that flanked the Sangre de Cristos north of Glorieta Pass.

Another rider was approaching, and Fargo reached, just to be sure his Sharps rifle and Colt revolver were at hand. But even though the man rode a short-legged Indian mustang, it was saddled regular and the rider's shout indicated that he wanted to be friendly.

Fargo relaxed even more when he recognized the grizzled man in buckskins as an old-time Taos trapper named Tigea O'Kilean. After they exchanged greetings, O'Kilean explained he was scouting the next campsite for a big wagon train a couple miles back.

Fargo explained his mission. "You must have ridden through there not long after it happened, Tige. How do you make it out?"

"Hell with the lid off, that's what it looked like when I come through. Wagons was just smokin' piles of ashes, 'bout all that was left was the stay bolts. Men all shot dead, scattered about. Dug some graves before the buzzards an' coyotes finished makin' dinner out of 'em. 'Bout all I could do."

"So you figure it was Comanche?" Fargo provoked.

"Jesus, Mary, and Joseph! By the great horned spoon, it wasn't Comanche. Why, Fargo, I never took you for no greenhorn, drippin' wet behind the ears. I always thought that, for a pup, you was pretty fair at this business. But boy, you're dumber'n a fencepost if that looked Comanche."

Satisfied that the old free trapper's love of bragging would tell him all he could possibly learn from O'Kilean, Fargo continued acting stupid. "From what I heard, it had to be Comanche."

"Then you was talkin' to folks that was idiots," O'Kilean jabbered. "Mr. Lo, he don't come without no warnin'. He'll shadow you, watch you, snipe at you some. He don't just ride up outta nowhere an' start shootin' away, not at no wagon train, anyway. So a train's allus got a chance to fort up. Or at least try. An' these wagons was still strung out in two lines, just like they was travelin'. They hadn't pulled 'em into a circle, an' they sure as sin would have if redskins had been ridin' up on 'em."

They dismounted, mostly to stretch, while O'Kilean lit his clay pipe.

"And if it'd been Comanche, then they'da done a better job of scalpin'. Never seen such clumsy, piss-poor work," the trapper complained. "Aside from that, there was nary an arrow in any of them bodies. Some Comanches carries guns. But always there's plenty with them short bows an' wicked arrows."

Fargo grunted his agreement, and O'Kilean continued. "Way I make it, they met up with folks that they thought was friends, an' them friends just rode in amidst the wagons an' then opened fire on 'em. After the killin' got done, they fired the wagons. The scalpin' was just done to make it look like an Injun raid, but it didn't fool me none."

"So maybe it was Comanchero." This talk of plains hazards was just making Fargo more observant than usual. He kept scanning the horizon, but all he noticed was a cloud of dust drawing closer, over behind another sagebrush-covered rise.

"More their style," O'Kilean conceded. "But them Comanchero is mostly breeds an' greasers, dressed not too different from Injun. Don't stand to reason that they could just ride in without raisin' suspicions."

And if there were suspicions, then every man in the wagon train would have been ready to fire, Fargo knew. He asked about tracks.

"Sure, there's tracks. God's plenty of tracks. There's tracks ever which way you might look out here. So many folks on the trail these days that the prairie looks like a damn sheep pen for all the tracks. There's buffalos wanderin' about, an' you might've noticed that the wind blows out here somethin' fearsome. For all that, you could just about as easy track the wind. Why, hell, even Jim Coulter couldn't track nobody here, an' that sumbitch . . . Well, let me tell you, him an' me was . . ."

Fargo turned his attention back to the cloud of dust. At its base was a lumbering ox-drawn wagon train, which had swung around the rise so that the lead wagons were now in direct sight, about a mile off. The big Murphy wagons came two abreast, a hundred feet between the rows, their canvas tops billowing with each little breeze and swaying with every bump. Most sounds were muffled, including the constant oaths of the bullwhackers, but Fargo could hear distinct pops, sharper sounds than even pistol reports, whenever they swung and cracked their long whips.

Caravans along the Santa Fe Trail always looked different than those along the other major trails of the West. Fargo had noticed that long ago, but it had taken him a while to figure out why. Along the other trails, there were emigrants, people setting out from Pennsylvania or Ohio to try to build a new life in Oregon or California.

Those folks never planned to repeat the journey. They packed stuff they didn't need and forgot things they did. They used draft horses when the trails required mules or oxen. They did a lot of things wrong, and too many of them died because they were either ignorant or too pigheaded to listen to more experienced folks.

But no matter how foolish the would-be settlers were, they had an energy, a surge of hope and ambition that you just never saw along the Santa Fe Trail.

Nobody ever took the Santa Fe Trail to build a new life somewhere. It was strictly a route of commerce, and the men who ran the wagon trains were professionals in a competitive business with a schedule to meet. Fargo appreciated their hard-won abilities, but he sometimes missed the enthusiasm of those greenhorn pioneers who had an adventure instead of just a job to do.

Fargo had done such a good job of closing his mind to O'Kilean's long-winded bragging that he didn't notice exactly when the old fart quit talking and started squinting, nervously looking back past the last wagon.

"Jesus Christ and John Jacob Astor," the trapper finally muttered. "What's happened to that damn-fool woman?"

As they remounted hurriedly and headed down the draw and up the next rise for a better view, O'Kilean explained the situation. Like many wagon trains, this one had been more or less assembled back in the middle of Kansas Territory, at Council Grove. Wagons rolled out from Missouri, a few at a time through well-watered land where the Indians were generally friendly. They halted at the westernmost stand of hardwoods, a spot called Council Grove, where there was oak and hickory for wagon repairs.

As soon as several dozen wagons were camped around Council Grove, they'd assemble, select a wagonmaster, and the train would start rolling west.

Among those bound for Santa Fe was a German merchant from Saint Louis who'd piled hardware in a wagon, with plans to triple his stake in Santa Fe. He'd also brought his *frau*, who got left with the wagon after Herr Kappelheimer caught the cholera somewhere near Point of Rock along the bone-dry gulch that mapmakers insisted on calling the Cimarron River.

"She's a haughty, standoffish one," O'Kilean said as they neared the top of the rise. "Takes no guff from anyone, and takes no help, neither. Her wagon ain't in the train."

Since Fargo didn't know her wagon from any of the others, he couldn't add much to the conversation, but after they topped the rise and saw nothing but ruts stretching eastward, and then started riding hard that way, he was reasonably sure that the busted-down wagon they finally saw was Hannah Kappelheimer's.

Fargo could tell in a glance what must have happened. The dry prairie air caused wood to shrink up, which pulled the wooden wheels away from their broad iron tires. Hannah Kappelheimer must have noticed that and halted so she could get out, cut some shims, and force the thin wedges in between the wheel and tire. Fargo could see some fresh shavings from her making shims, along with her footprints in the hard ground and the tracks of three or four unshod ponies.

While she was standing next to the wagon, hammering in the shims, the wagon train rolled on, over a little swell, just high enough to be out of sight. The wind was coming from that way, carrying sounds off to where no one was listening when the Indians who shaded every wagon train, looking for loose livestock, found a straggler along with three yoke of oxen.

Somewhere within thirty miles, Fargo knew, there would be a feast tonight. And likely a party, at which Hannah Kappelheimer would get passed from brave to brave, until she died, bleeding and in screaming agony, sometime tomorrow or the next day.

That wasn't always the case, Fargo reminded himself. Some chief might take a shine to her, in which case she'd live about as well as any Comanche woman did. Which wasn't saying much. It was a nomadic tribe where the men all rode horses, and all the women walked, carrying

76

everything that had to be carried for hundreds of desert miles.

When the two men finished circling the wagon for sign, Fargo noticed that O'Kilean's bluster had vanished. They met face to face, wordless because neither man wanted to talk about what had just happened.

"That contrary she-male," O'Kilean finally muttered. "Sure as shit stinks somebody offered to stay back an' help her, and she shooed 'em on. Just her way, I reckon."

Fargo quietly stepped toward the Ovaro.

"Want to fetch some help from the train?" O'Kilean asked.

Fargo shook his head, hating the way that the sweat rolled down his forehead, gathering trail dust to become mud for his eyes. Time was what mattered here. It had been a small raiding party, four braves, and Fargo knew there was a fighting chance if he could catch up to them before they got back to the main band.

The Indians couldn't have much more than an hour's start on them, and Fargo knew that his Ovaro, even with the trailing mule, was more than a match for their ponies. His horseflesh got grained and watered every night, whereas the Comanche weren't nearly so thoughtful.

Subsisting on prairie grass, their ponies didn't have much staying power, although that seldom bothered the Comanche. Whenever one horse gave out, they'd just steal another one. Or another fifty.

Fargo and Tige rode east, proceeding into their lengthening shadows. Fargo studied the ground, learning what he could from fresh hootprints in the sandy soil that spread before them, punctuated by sagebrush, yucca, and creosote bush.

One set of pony tracks sank deeper than the others, which stood to reason if somebody was riding double on account of Hannah Kappelheimer. From the length of the pony strides, indicating an easy trot, Fargo deduced the Indians weren't in any special hurry. That could be explained by all the hoofmarks of oxen tracks among the pony tracks. Even the Comanche had never figured out a way to move cattle fast.

But that worried Fargo. Indians who came upon a few

available steers generally butchered them right on the spot. It was easier to bring the tribe to the feast than to bring the meal to the camp. So if this little warrior band decided to herd the six oxen, it meant that their main camp couldn't be too far away. As if he were able to read Fargo's mind, the Ovaro quickened his trot, and if the mule minded, it didn't do anything about it.

They had to be getting close now, which forced a change in their approach. Cresting a hilltop, with the sun right behind you, made you into a prominent target. So Fargo and O'Kilean split at each rise to flank the high points and rejoin as they dropped. At one of these draws, it stood to reason that the Indians would turn and follow the draw one way or the other, instead of continuing cross-country over hill and dale.

O'Kilean was out of Fargo's sight, over on the left somewhere, when Fargo heard the whoops and shots. He swung the Ovaro hard that way, staying as low as he could. The noises got louder and louder, but Fargo still couldn't see the action. Knowing that it all had to be happening over the little swell before him, Fargo dismounted and crawled up to its gentle crest.

Sharps in hand and cactus in his chest, Fargo eyed the predicament that was developing about two hundred yards away.

O'Kilean had just about ridden into the band of Comanche raiders. Before he could do much about it, they'd spotted him. Three were now pursuing him back up the hillside, while the fourth, the one riding double with Hannah Kappelheimer, just sat on his horse over on the other side of the brushy draw, amid the oxen.

The gap between them and O'Kilean was less than a hundred yards. Fargo got the Sharps into shooting position, but all he would do was waste lead and draw attention to himself if he tried to shoot at targets that were weaving and moving so quickly. Taking out the Indian with Hannah was an appealing idea, but at that range, he couldn't be positive that he'd hit the brave instead of the woman.

Maybe O'Kilean didn't know everything he said he did, but the old man knew something about plains warfare. When it was obvious that he wasn't going to outrun the three warriors, he savagely jerked his mount to a skidding halt. Leaping off, he pulled his monstrous belt knife and slit the quivering animal's throat.

The pony twitched and fell, O'Kilean pushing the carcass so it landed between him and the approaching Indians. The old trapper dropped behind the still-bleeding barricade.

Since the Comanche never spent much time training the horses they stole, their ponies never got over an instinctive hatred for the smell of fresh blood. The braves were about thirty yards off, still charging hard and whooping as they came, when their mounts caught wind of the odor they detested.

The mounts instantly reared and twisted, and it was all the Indians could manage to stay aboard. Even when the horses settled some, nothing would persuade them to come any closer to O'Kilean, who was hunkered down there with a carbine and three feet of warm flesh to protect him from such bullets as the Comanche were able to fire from their single antique fusil rifle.

When the brave with the rifle brought it up to his shoulder, O'Kilean's carbine barked, and the old trapper wouldn't have to worry about any more Indian bullets for a while.

Arrows were a different story. Bullets went in straight lines, but a good archer could make an arrow arc over a low barricade and annoy the hell out of whoever was behind it. And the Comanche were good archers.

O'Kilean's carbine knocked one warrior right off his horse when the man was trying to fetch some more arrows from his quiver. The other warrior was circling, trying to get over to the side where he'd have a better shot.

He was himself an impossible shot for the old trapper. He'd twisted his lithe red body so that his torso was along the far side of the horse, leaving only a leg as a target. The brave leaned far forward, ready to bend even farther down and loose his arrows from beneath the horse's neck. If Fargo hadn't seen it done before, he wouldn't have thought it was possible.

From Fargo's hidden vantage, though, the Comanche presented a fair target for his Sharps. The warrior was no doubt confused and full of questions when he arrived at the Happy Hunting Grounds a moment after riding into Fargo's sights.

At that, the double-mounted brave on the other side of the draw decided he'd seen enough, and took off for wherever he'd been going. He didn't even pause to see if the oxen wanted to come along with him and Hannah.

Fargo stood as O'Kilean looked up, hollered something exuberant, and waved him toward the departing brave. Fargo ran down the hillside the way he'd come, and jumped aboard the Ovaro. Old Tige, with three horses to pick from to replace his mount, would be along whenever.

Fargo figured he had maybe fifteen minutes of good light remaining before the scarlet sun sank behind the western mountains and washed their summits with a blood-colored glow that long ago had provided the Spanish name for the range: Sangre de Cristo, which meant "blood of Christ."

Rescuing Hannah Kappelheimer turned out to be about what Fargo thought it would be. He crested the next rise and noticed that the brush below was thicker than any he'd seen in this neighborhood. So that draw was wetter than most, which meant there must be some real water farther down. If the Comanche camp was as near as it had to be, it would be by that water. There wasn't any other place for it.

Fargo stayed out of the bottomland, riding just below the flank in the open ground. The Comanche kidnapper would stay in the brush, trusting his stealth to get him and his captive back to camp. Fargo's sensitive ears picked up some unavoidable noises from down that way, but he pressed on ahead, finally stopping above a clear spot in the draw, where there was a muddy pool, one almost too big to jump across. It wasn't much more than a puddle, but it was the first water Fargo had seen all day.

In the dimming twilight, he dismounted and strolled down the hillside, Colt in hand. At first, he'd thought about waiting up on the hill and picking off the brave when he rode by. But it was getting too dark for accurate shooting at that range.

Besides, when two people were on a horse and you wanted to hit only one of them while saving the other, too many things could go wrong. Horses could move and shift their passengers in the brief interval between the squeezing of a trigger and the arrival of a .50-caliber Sharps bullet. Another possible complication was that the Sharps was built for hunting buffalo, which were considerably thicker than humans. A bullet that stopped in the middle of a shaggy bull could sail on right through a man and also kill the woman sitting behind him.

Fargo made himself comfortable in the brush on the downhill side of the pool. About fifteen minutes later, he heard some rustling, then a pause. Moving gently, he adjusted his perch and saw what he thought he'd see. The brave was on foot, taking a leak, while the horse bent down to quench its thirst.

Bound and gagged, her china-doll eyes scrunched shut, Hannah Kappelheimer sat uncomfortably on the horse's back, her feet tied underneath by a rawhide rope. She couldn't have been very tall, because her feet were still quite a ways apart, and the pony wasn't all that big.

There must have been some noise when Fargo brought his revolver up, because the bowlegged Comanche warrior did start to turn his way when Fargo's bullet caught the man in the ribs. He let out a whoop that halted instantly when Fargo's second bullet entered his ear, coming out the other side in a spray of blood and brain that annoyed hell out of the pony.

In a leap, Fargo was across the tiny pool, his big hand on the hair bridle. Pull as he might, the critter didn't want to settle down, so Fargo rolled his other arm around the horse's neck and got aboard. Once the pony understood that they were going away from all that awful fresh blood, he became cooperative and was almost friendly by the time they got up the hill to the Ovaro and the mule, and didn't mind a bit when Fargo got off, cut the rawhide thong that bound her feet, and lifted Hannah Kappelheimer off.

She was rescued, but she hadn't figured that out yet.

Wide-eyed and terrified, she kicked all the way down and started to run off after Fargo put her feet on the ground. Knife still in hand, he easily caught her from behind, clamping her shoulder with one hand while wondering how to slit her wrist bonds without nicking her. It was getting to be as dark as the inside of a cow, and she was wriggling and twisting like a snake in a hurry.

Perhaps some explanation would help, but before Fargo could say anything, the sky lit up as a sheet of lightning cracked across the sky, followed by roll after roll of thunder. Not a drop of rain was falling, though. It was one of those dry thunderstorms that made prairie life so interesting and prairie death so frequent.

"Excuse me," Fargo finally shouted during a lull. "All I want to do is get you back to your wagon train. I don't aim to abuse you."

She turned some under his grip, and he got his first good look at her in the frozen blue glare of the next flash from the sky. Change her coloring some, and she could have passed for a Comanche squaw; she had the same sort of short, husky build. Under normal light, her pinned-up hair would be blond, rather than the eerie white it was under the lightning. She looked frightened, and it was unlikely she'd believe that Fargo offered anything better than the Comanche had. As far as she was concerned, he was just another kidnapper.

Fargo pulled her around, wrapped both his arms behind her, and managed to free her hands without damaging her. Which was likely a mistake, because she seemed to think that he'd done that just so she could claw at his face. He revised his grip to pin her arms to her heaving sides, feeling kind of foolish, standing there wrestling with, and trying to talk to, a terrified woman who still had a gag jammed in her mouth.

He bent down so that he wouldn't be talking to the bun atop her head. "Will you listen for a goddamn minute?" he started, and broke off in midsentence as her skirt-clad knee came up and jabbed him in the balls. His grip relaxed and she wiggled, spun, and took off again.

Gritting his teeth and wondering about his sanity, Fargo next saw her, illuminated by lightning, loping down the hillside toward the horses, who'd moved down some because they didn't want to be any closer to the flashing sky than they had to be.

He started that way. The next bolt showed her next to the Comanche pony, trying to get on. That image remained frozen in Fargo's consciousness for only a moment, to be replaced by the sight of a fleeing horse, kicking up its heels, and Hannah Kappelheimer sprawled face-first on the ground.

Momentarily envying the horse for its good sense in running away from this wildcat, Fargo knelt next to her and undid the gag. Pulling her up by her shoulders to a sitting position, he could tell she was still breathing, although another flash showed that her nose was bloody. He fetched a bandanna out of his hip pocket and wiped the stunned woman's face until she started shaking her head.

"Will you just sit still and listen for a minute or two?" Fargo shouted. "I'm not going to hurt you."

He felt her shudder, and when the thunder quieted a bit, he heard great gasping sobs. Finally she caught her breath, "Vat do you vant from me?"

"To stay put, ma'am. To quit running off. To listen for a spell. You're going to get us both hurt if you keep this up. You understand?"

"Ja." She seemed to slump under Fargo's hands, which he removed from her soft shoulders.

"Okay," Fargo told her. "I've got a horse and a mule that are tired and thirsty, and I've got to tend to them. Then I've got to figure out just where we're going to set up tonight, and get us fed. First light tomorrow, I'll get you back to your wagon train. You got that?"

"Verstaht das gut," she said, then caught herself. "You vant me to stay right here while you care for the horses, *ja?"*

"Ja," Fargo said, getting onto his feet, wondering if he needed to tie her up again.

But she was still sitting there when he returned half an hour later after unsaddling the mule and his Ovaro, which looked eerie in the lightning. His jet-black fore and hind quarters just stayed invisible while the white midsection almost glowed. He looked like only part of a horse. As for the mule, every time there was a flash, it looked like what Fargo thought a ghost mule should look like, all gray and indistinct.

There were anthills where Hannah sat, which meant this was as good a place as any to stay through a dry thunderstorm. It might not be raining here, but it sure could be pouring to the west. And if that was the case, then sometime during the night, a wall of seething water could surge down this ravine. It was amazing how many people drowned in the desert, just because they didn't camp high enough. They didn't even think about it, because it wasn't raining where they were.

Ants went to a lot of work to build their colonies, and they didn't like to lose all that toil to flash floods. So if there were anthills in a spot, it was unlikely to get very wet.

But it didn't pay to get too high during these storms, either, on account of lightning. All along these sandy ridges, an observant man could spot bizarre red-and-black chains, formed when the heat of a bolt from the sky had fused the sand grains together.

That was also what made riding anywhere tonight a foolish notion. Lightning generally hit the high points, and in this treeless region, a man on a horse was about as high as anything those thunderbolts were likely to find.

Hannah finally loosened up and started to talk some while Fargo fished some jerky and cornmeal out of a pannier, along with a canteen he'd filled with decent water early that morning, which seemed like an aeon ago.

After her husband's feverish death, Hannah had decided to go on to Santa Fe because she didn't see as she had much choice. From what she'd heard, even someone like her, who didn't know a lot about running a hardware store, could at least triple her investment there. If she'd taken the wares back to Saint Louis, she'd have been lucky to come out even.

Men on wagon trains being like men anywhere else, she got lots of offers to help whenever she ran into a problem.

"But den dey vould stand behind me ven I vas trying to do someting," she explained. "Unt dey vould rub my behint mit der fronts. Dey vould bring arms arount to put hands on, how do you zay it, my bosom?"

When the sky lit up momentarily, Fargo got a good idea of the twin attractions as she sat on a saddle blanket, facing him. Her bosom did look mighty pleasant to put one's hands on. The short woman was a bit on the chubby side, but her padding tended to settle in the right places. He chewed on his jerky thoughtfully as she continued.

"Zo I chust run them off. They no help at all. Ven I vant help, I vant help. Ven I vant man, I vant man. I don't vant both at same time. That why no one stay to help me ven das veel get loose and Indians take me." She halted for a swallow from the canteen. "And I thought you chust another man that want to . . ."

Fargo would have been lying if he had said he didn't want to, but he thought it best to change the subject. No sense talking about and thinking about things that weren't likely to happen. He cleared his throat to interrupt her, and stood up.

"Time to bed down for the night," he announced, grabbing the bedroll and opening it, "You can sleep in this bedroll. I'll need that saddle blanket you're sitting on."

"But, Herr Fargo," she protested, "it is not right that you should zleep like that. It is your bedroll and you must use it."

"No, ma'am," Fargo objected. "You've had all the trouble you need for one day, and you just crawl inside that bedroll and get yourself a good night's sleep. I'll be nearby, just to make sure no menfolk try to bother you."

For the first time since they'd met, she laughed. "Herr Fargo, you sure you vish to zleep alone?"

This woman was exasperating as hell, whether she was tied up and gagged, or loose and talking. Fargo decided to make matters as clear as he could without offending any delicate sensibilities the woman might harbor. "Look, if I'm in that bedroll with you, something might happen."

He paused for a moment, trying to make sure he was

really seeing what he thought he saw when the lightning went off. She had stood and undone her simple cotton dress, which lay in a ring around her stockinged feet.

A moment later, the instant of light showed that her chemise had dropped. She stood there, pale and ethereal, a hand cupped under each of her plump breasts. "Do you not vish to enjoy dese, Herr Fargo? Honest, zir, I do not vish to zleep alone tonight. It would frighten me mitout a strong man at my side."

Fargo was kind of tired with arguing with Hannah, so he figured it was time to be agreeable. By the time he shucked his duds and crawled inside the warm bedroll, she was more than ready, her soft arms and legs instantly entwining him as he thrust in deeply.

Silent except for her feverish panting, Hannah Kappelheimer seemed to grow under him, enveloping him in a dewy softness that absorbed plunge after plunge. After a dry, harsh day, Fargo found ecstasy in every little sensation. The way her nipples bored into his chest, moving with him as her underlying breasts vibrated. The surprising sleekness of her thighs as they spread further and further. The way her bottom responded to his grip as he pulled himself in deeper and deeper. The way she let loose, all grasping arms and flying legs, when he went off at just the same moment as the biggest thunderclap of the night.

5

After a hard day and a hard night in various saddles, the last thing Fargo wanted to do was rise before the sun. But the storm had blown by so that a dozen or so of the brighter stars were twinkling in the clear sky, and the dawn was just a gray promise along the horizon when he made his way back toward camp.

His early exploratory walk had taken him about two miles down along the twisting draw. Staying close to the crest of its flank, but a few yards below so that he wouldn't show up in anyone's skyline view, Fargo had gone far enough to see what he didn't want to see: a big Comanche camp with dozens of tepees and a horse herd that would be counted in the hundreds.

Once the Indians started stirring this morning, they'd be on the prod, since at least one horse had come back yesterday without its rider. They'd be out looking for the source of trouble. There was absolutely no chance of hiding from the Comanche. Miserable as this land was, it was their home, and they knew it intimately.

By himself, Fargo wouldn't have any trouble hopping aboard the Ovaro and outrunning any Indians who might want to settle up for yesterday. Hannah's presence complicated matters.

If they rode double, the Ovaro probably couldn't stay ahead of the Comanche. Putting Hannah on the mule might work, except that would mean jettisoning most of the supplies, supplies they might well need; dying of starvation or thirst wasn't much of an improvement over slow torture from the Comanches.

They weren't more than ten or fifteen miles from the Santa Fe Trail, which they might reach before the Comanche caught up to them, but there sure as hell weren't any guarantees that there would be help waiting at the trail. O'Kilean might have returned to the wagon train and recruited a rescue expedition, but then again, the old trapper might have decided to stay on the job once he got back. If he got back at all.

Whatever they did, they'd need water, so Fargo stopped, enjoyed a moment's glance at Hannah sleeping peacefully with a big smile, and rounded up the canteens for a trip down to the muddy pool. The best that could be said for that water was that it was wet. It was warm and brackish, and full of wriggling critters that Fargo tried to strain out with a worn piece of an old blanket.

While he knelt at the muddy edge, he saw that the pool had been a busy spot last night, the way that all water in dry regions attracted a crowd. The Ovaro and the mule had come down to drink at least twice, leaving footprints. There were also some small antelope tracks, as well as some coyote prints. The coyotes, though, had found the stiff body of the brave as interesting as the water, and had chewed some on his legs.

On the far side of the pool were some big tracks. From Fargo's vantage, they looked like the impressions made by the broad hooves of a draft horse, maybe a Percheron or a Belgian. But there weren't any farms hereabouts that needed plow animals, and those immense brutes required too much grain and water to be of any use pulling wagons across the desert.

Curious, Fargo stepped around the pool for a better look. Up close, the indentations in the mud were even more perplexing. They were hoof marks, sure enough. No sign of claws or pads. And they were split, more or less like a buffalo hoof. But the prints were huge, bigger than Fargo's hand.

Telling himself that he was a damned fool for not rousing Hannah and moving out toward the trail as quickly as possible, Fargo followed the footprints up the sandy ground toward the top of the rise. That, he allowed, was as far as he'd go to satisfy curiosity before tending to more serious business, like staying alive and out of Comanche hands. He glanced back at the camp, fixing its location as best he could in a land without landmarks, and crossed the gentle rise to see what he could see.

What he saw down in the hollow was something he'd seen only once before, in a circus long ago. A skinny-legged beast with big hooves, a long shaggy neck, and a hump on its back. A camel, just standing there and sleeping as if it belonged there.

Hunkering his way slowly down the slope to get a better look, Fargo tried to figure out why a camel would be roaming around New Mexico, and then recalled a recent campfire story that he'd dismissed as a tall tale.

As the story went, the U.S. Army had trouble supplying its forts strung along the southwestern desert. Since folks that lived in other big deserts had solved similar problems with camels—they could carry better than seven hundred pounds apiece, eat anything that grew, and go for a week or so without water—the army had imported thirty-three of the beasts back in 1856, and tested them on a pack trip from Texas to California and back again.

From what Fargo had heard, the camels had performed magnificently, although the imported beasts needed imported Turkish handlers because few Americans knew beans about getting camels to obey orders.

The main problem, though, was that everyone that a camel caravan encountered used horses, donkeys, or mules, which all hated the way camels smelled. The members of the horse family responded by getting frisky as all hell in their haste to get away from the vile odor of the dromedaries. Camels were also foul-tempered and spit at everything within range. Being spit on had to be an improvement on being kicked, which was what foul-tempered mules did to everything they thought they might reach.

Creeping up closer, and knowing he should lope back to camp and start tending to business, Fargo allowed that the old boy who'd told the story must not have been stretching the truth all that much. The camel definitely bore a "US" brand on its tan flank, and it was still wearing a bridle. This one had probably wandered off from Fort Fillmore, down by Las Cruces, the supply depot for the desert forts that spread westward to California.

Now, within a couple yards of the camel, Fargo tried to talk himself out of the notion that kept running through his head. He couldn't, so in one smooth motion he grabbed the reins and started barking all the harsh, guttural sounds he could muster. Fargo was a big man, but not big enough to mount a camel without the animal's cooperation.

Some combination of Fargo's shouted consonants must have appealed to the camel, because it soon knelt. Fargo got aboard, spraddling the beast's withers as he gained a perch between neck and hump.

With a few more grunts that sounded like awful cussing, Fargo dug his heels into the camel's muscled shoulders and felt it rise.

For a few moments, Fargo thought the camel was going through the customary disagreements about who was boss. He wondered how on earth he'd stay aboard with no stirrups or saddle. But then he realized that his stomach was swaying on account of the peculiar stench. And because he was sitting so much higher than usual. And because the camel had an odd gait. It walked like a cat, sending both right legs forward, then both left legs.

Other than that, riding a camel wasn't too different from riding anything else. The animal steered just like a hard-mouthed horse, so Fargo put some pull on the reins and headed for the Comanche camp, gaining speed as he and the camel got used to each other.

Most of the village was still sleeping, although the sentries were awake enough to feel dumbfounded when the camel pounded by and their ponies' nostrils flared. The alarmed horses suddenly started trying to turn themselves inside out. Comanche warriors were great horsemen, perhaps the best there ever were, but even they couldn't stay in control.

Both nearby sentries, still mystified by the bizarre beast they had seen, got thrown into the cactus as their mounts took off for Texas or someplace even farther east. Wherever they were going, they were sure in a hurry to get there.

Fargo looped to get upwind of the huge horse herd

before swinging straight toward it. He was still a quarter-mile off when the ponies caught wind of what was coming and decided they didn't want anything to do with it.

From the Trailsman's high perch, it looked like an explosion in the herd. It started with a wave of bucking and pitching that began on his side and worked back. Then hooves started glinting in the day's first sunlight as the terrified horses reared and pawed at the air.

Fargo and the camel drove closer. The Comanche horses totally forgot their manners. They stampeded in a great surge, directly toward the encampment. A few squaws that were up early fixing breakfast or whatever raced back into their teepees as the horses thundered through, knocking over cook fires and hide-tanning frames.

When all that remained of the herd was a vast cloud of slowly settling dust, Fargo turned the camel toward his own camp. More than most Indians, the Comanche hated to be afoot. For the next three or four days, or maybe even longer than that, they'd be a lot more concerned with putting their herd back together than with bothering Fargo. Even getting to their herd would take a while, because there wasn't even one horse remaining in sight of the Indian camp.

Somewhat apprehensive as to whether the rest of his idea would work, Fargo tied his humped mount to a creosote bush near where they'd met, and ambled over the little rise, across the gulch, and back to camp. A worried Hannah was up and about, reassembling the bedroll after they'd disturbed it considerable during their pleasure last night.

"Ach, Herr Fargo, vat ist it dat you haf been doing?" she exclaimed as soon as he got within earshot.

Fargo couldn't think of any easy way to explain, and such sweet talking as he had in him this morning should be reserved for the Ovaro, who wasn't going to like his plan much at all. So he just grunted something about morning chores and gave Hannah a peck on an upper cheek and a pinch on a lower cheek. She appeared to enjoy them both.

In fifteen minutes, the Ovaro and mule were ready to travel. The mule was tethered by a lead rope attached to

Fargo's riding saddle, and Fargo had found enough odds and ends to blindfold the mule.

The best way to put the mule on good behavior for what came next would have been to cover its nose instead of its eyes, but Fargo couldn't see any way to do that and still allow the brute to breathe. The Ovaro's nostrils flared and he got huffy as soon as Fargo led them all, a curious Hannah included, over to the camel and explained that they all had to be friends for the next two or three days, until they got to Fort Union, over on the mountain branch of the Santa Fe Trail.

Fargo felt kind of obligated to both Hannah and the camel, but with them along, he couldn't even get a good start on the job he'd come out here to do.

Fort Union looked like the safest place to leave them both. The camel, after all, was government property, and Fargo figured he might as well try to be a good citizen and return it to the nearest government installation. As for Hannah, she could certainly catch a ride to either Santa Fe or Saint Louis from there. Her oxen were scattered, and even if this part of the world looked unpopulated, anything valuable left in an abandoned wagon still managed to disappear.

They made a curious procession. Aboard the swaying camel, Fargo was developing blisters and sores in new places as he rode along, generally staying abreast with Hannah atop the Ovaro. Holding the saddle horn most of the time like the tenderfoot she was, she rode gingerly; Fargo's stirrups just couldn't be shortened enough so that her feet could reach them. The pack mule had its complaints about being so near to a camel, but the blindfold kept it from doing too much about its objections.

Still uncertain as to just which grunts made the camel kneel and get up, Fargo wasn't about to dismount any more often than he had to. So the other five men in the oncoming party stayed mounted and a ways off when Tigea O'Kilean saw Fargo's short caravan and discovered that if he wanted to get close enough to talk, he'd have to walk over.

The old trapper fought off an attack of laughter for long enough to tell Fargo the obvious—that he'd borrowed a Comanche pony and hightailed it back to the wagon train last night. By then the darkness and lightning made it foolish to go looking for Fargo and the damn-fool woman, but first thing this morning they'd headed out to help if they could.

"It sure do shine, Fargo," he concluded, "to see the both of you with your hair still on. But where in tarnation did you find that peculiar chunk of horseflesh? Goddamn thing looks like it was put together by a government committee."

Looking down at O'Kilean's upturned and weathered face, Fargo didn't elaborate too much on his skills as a camel tamer, and he didn't need to exaggerate at all about what happened to the Comanche herd when he rode up on his dreadful dromedary. That settled, Fargo explained his destination. O'Kilean whooped and scuttled back to his horse as fast as his bandy legs would carry him, in a hurry to tell a new tale that he was already starting to embroider on.

Skye Fargo and Hannah Kappelheimer didn't see any more people that day, nor that night, during which they had to slow down twice to reassemble the bedroll, nor the next day until well in the afternoon, as Fargo squinted into the sun, knew that they were almost into the mountains, and wondered just how much farther Fort Union could possibly be.

The next person they saw was just some private on picket duty, whose eyes grew big and even bigger before waving them on toward the fort, a cluster of ramshackle buildings sitting in the middle of a treeless expanse. Some were wood and some were adobe, and all were in poor repair. Good thing it didn't rain much in these parts.

The remount officer's broad sunburned face had more furrows than a plowed field as he stared down at the dog-eared volume of regulations on his desk before returning his gaze to Fargo.

"Shore an' begorra, I know it's my damn job to make sure Uncle Sam's mounts gets taken care of," Lieutenant Aloysius Murphy agreed in his deep brogue, "but Uncle Sam never told me nothin' about such brutes as you came bringing in."

Fargo just nodded in commiseration and resumed his inspection of the patterns that the flies were forming on the whitewashed plank wall behind Murphy's desk.

The husky lieutenant's face twisted a few more times as he pawed through the book. "Jayzus," he finally exclaimed. "There's nothin' in the book concernin' such beasties. Supposin' we tend him like a horse, keepin' him away from the others, of course, till I can round up one of them heathen Turks to take the beastie off our hands?"

That sounded like a question, so Fargo answered that it seemed reasonable as far as he was concerned. He cautioned that camels had a reputation for being temperamental and touchy to work around, and excused himself.

The army was making up for its inept camel tenders, Fargo discovered when he entered post headquarters. Whatever skilled attention the camel lacked, the adjutant was more than making up for on Hannah.

Fargo suspected that Major Henry Staub had been Heinrich Staub not all that long ago, from the way he and Hannah were chattering away in German. From the moonstruck way that the rail-thin blond officer looked at her, and her fluttering doe eyes in response, Fargo also suspected that Hannah Kappelheimer would soon be Frau Staub if nature took its course. And he had no intention of disturbing nature.

The tanned man reddened some when he finally noticed that he and Hannah were no longer alone in the room. He'd been sitting next to her on a splintery bench, and rose to shake hands.

"You'd be Mr. Fargo, the man that brought in the camel." Fargo pumped his bony hand and nodded. "The old man said he'd like to see you as soon as you're ready."

"Now's as good a time as any, I reckon."

Staub pointed down the shadowy hall and said Colonel E.R.S. Canby's office was the last one on the left.

Fargo had hoped that the colonel might know something about the raid on that had wiped out a wagon train and killed Hank Barclay, but either Canby knew less than Fargo did or else he was playing his cards mighty close to his vest.

Unsatisfied, Fargo checked his assigned quarters in the guest barracks and saw that his cot and room held no more lice than could be expected. He replenished his supplies at the post sutler's and then messed with the officers, who wanted to ask about Hannah but couldn't, since Major Staub glared at them every time she was mentioned. So they talked about camels through most of dinner, some stringy beef cooked a lot more than it needed to be.

Fargo hadn't learned a damn thing at Fort Union about the Barclay Massacre, but he wasn't giving up. Like every military installation he'd ever seen, Fort Union supported a nearby settlement where soldiers could spend their pay. They could guzzle whiskey that might blind them, gamble in rigged games, and find themselves knocked cold and robbed after taking up a painted-up gal's offer of three ways for a dollar.

Of the three false-fronted saloons, Fargo picked the biggest and worst-looking, correctly surmising that it would be where the enlisted men drank. Unlike the officers, the cavalry troopers actually knew something about events along the trail. And since Fargo was buying, they were more than willing to gossip.

Fargo and the dozen or so privates, corporals, and sergeants gathered around the table were into their third bottle of whiskey. He'd learned that the Barclay Massacre was pretty much a mystery to them, too, although they had some theories that sounded sensible.

Up the mountain branch of the Santa Fe Trail, about two days' ride north of the fort, was the settlement of Cimarron. Fargo remembered it fondly as home of a brewery whose beer he liked. But the front end of the stone building held one of the roughest dives in the West, Swink's Saloon, where deadly gunfights occurred almost nightly.

"There's some new bunch of hard cases up there," a private explained, "and there's talk that they've been pretty much riding and robbing however they please. There's a couple of 'em in the stockade right now."

"How'd they get there?" Fargo asked, his attention now focused.

"Stupidity," a corporal answered. "I'll give you a little advice, though I doubt you need it. Next time you set up camp somewhere, don't set it up next to a military beef herd if you've got runnin' irons in your gear."

"What's going happen to them?" Fargo inquired.

"Hard to say," the corporal said after draining his shot glass and pouring some more red-eye, his hand surprisingly steady, given that it was fourth or fifth round in about an hour. "It's up to the old man, and he's got other fish to fry right now. Can't court-martial 'em, 'cause they're not soldiers. Maybe they oughtta go to Santa Fe to the territorial court, but that's a lot of trouble. The longer they stay here, the more exciting things might get, though."

"Why's that?" Fargo poured himself some more whiskey, although his glass was only half-empty. It was one way to make people think you were drinking more than you really were, when you wanted them to get a little loose while staying in control of your own wits.

"Oh, shit, there's talk that their gang might ride down here an' bust 'em out."

"Most of that gang up in Cimarron," a burly sergeant broke in, "are the same riffraff that's been around here forever. But it used to be that some was here, some was in Taos, some in Santa Fe, an' so forth. Now the whole lot of 'em's hanging out at Swink's Saloon."

"Any idea why?" Fargo asked.

"Your guess is as good as mine," the sergeant answered. "With all the Indians here, we ain't had much time for chasin' no outlaws. An' besides, that ain't no real army job nohow. S'posed to be up to them civilians over in the territorial marshal's office to get folks to obey the law." They all started laughing, since the New Mexico Territorial Marshal's office was known from Missouri to California as a haven for political appointees and other crooked sorts.

They were just catching their breath when their easy-going bourbon-fueled joviality was shattered. Out of the corner of his eye, Fargo saw a sergeant who'd staked out a nearby table to himself rise and start his way. There were two good reasons that the man had been sitting

96

alone: one was that he was big enough to need his own private table, and the other was that he was so surly that nobody wanted to drink with him anyway.

Fargo had taken his usual saloon seat—his back against the wall where he could see the door—but this time it wasn't working for him. When the red-bearded goliath brought down an immense hand, Fargo had nowhere to twist before it clamped his shoulder.

The livid-faced giant was just standing there looking proddy while the place got real quiet, so Fargo finally asked just what his problem was.

"I ain't the one with a problem, you yellow-bellied sissy. Why come you ain't servin' your country? You chickenshit or what?"

If that's what the army was using for recruiting officers these days, Fargo thought, then it wasn't any wonder that he'd turned a deaf ear to the bugle's call and hadn't enlisted.

Fargo glanced around the table, trying to read the faces, and quickly understood their predicament. Skye Fargo was a much more likable fellow than this lumbering oaf. But the oaf wore the same uniform as they did, which meant they couldn't really take sides against him. And Fargo would ride on, whereas they'd have to deal with this gargantuan creature every day for months, perhaps years. Neutrality was all Fargo had any right to expect; he saw that he'd get that, but no more. They'd stay out of whatever developed.

"Hey, now," Fargo cautioned, "ask your buddies here. I did serve my country today. I brought back a government camel, didn't I?"

There were a couple of nervous sniggers, but it was obvious that Fargo's opinions didn't count for a lot anymore.

"Wait a minute," Fargo protested. "I've done scouting for the army. For Major Carl Whitsted, up in Montana."

The pressure increased on Fargo's shoulder. "I was in that outfit." Fargo did recall a man in that cavalry troop that looked bigger than many of the horses, but the fellow had been clean-shaven then. "You didn't impress me much then, and now I figure you're a goddamn slacker."

Fargo shook his head while thinking, which was depressing. This huge creature had all the advantage. Even if Fargo reached down for his Colt, the big man could get that massive hand around Fargo's neck and start causing real damage long before the Trailsman could get his hand under the table and get the gun out to where he might do something with it.

"Whose side you on, Fargo? Injuns? Mexicans?"

Hard as it was, Fargo pushed a big grin across his face. "Skye Fargo's side, asshole." Fargo punctuated the statement by jabbing his elbow, hard and fast as he could, into the man's crotch.

He grunted and folded a little, bringing his chin down within Fargo's reach. Fargo brought up his fist to slam the sergeant's fleshy jaw, his arm stinging with the force of impact as the man's head rocked back against the wall.

That had taken only moments, which was long enough for the men who'd been sitting around the table to get somewhere else. Fargo sidled away, discouraging his opponent's lunge by pushing his chair into the man's tree-trunk legs. The sergeant responded by getting tangled in the chair and losing his footing. His immense torso crashed down on the table, with enough force to shatter at least two of its flimsy wooden legs.

Just to be on the safe side, Fargo grabbed one of those table legs as it flew out, and used it to club the pumpkin-sized red head. The furious kicking stopped; the man's blue eyes blinked at the ceiling several times, and then closed with a groan.

The bartender, an oily fellow who'd been clutching a greener thoughtfully, muttered something about the foolishness of anyone who made a living selling whiskey to soldiers. Instead of putting the shotgun down after the ruckus settled, he waved it Fargo's way and explained that Fargo had worn out his welcome at the Exchange Saloon.

Fargo didn't see any cause to argue with the man's sentiments or the two yawning barrels of his eight-gauge.

He had business elsewhere tonight, and after all, there were two other saloons to try if fate ever brought him through here again.

Stomping down the boardwalk toward the Ovaro, Fargo studied on just how he was going to see the two men in the stockade. He had some questions to ask them, and he didn't see that he'd be getting much more help from the officers and men of Fort Union. Even at that, dealing with two men would be simpler than riding up to Cimarron and wandering into a saloon full of hard cases.

"Hey, handsome," came the whisper from a shadowed doorway. "Lookin' for some fun?"

"Are you?" Fargo stepped right into the shadow, where the overwhelming odor of powder and perfume almost gagged him. Even though he could see only by such light as the saloon across the street gave off, he sure enjoyed looking down at the pair of pearly globes that her low-cut dress displayed to advantage.

She looked up at Fargo, licking her cupid's-bow lips with a tongue that flitted like a rattler's. "I give great French lessons, handsome." She pressed her lithe body against Fargo and rubbed some.

Fargo had often suspected that there was a connection in men that ran straight from the eyes to the groin, missing the brain entirely. It was the only way to explain how men, himself included, so often got themselves in trouble when around women like this one. Struggling to make sure his brain remained in charge despite the yearning in his loins, Fargo rested his arm on her bare shoulders and let his fingertips trail down the smooth flesh to the upper swell of her bosom.

"How's business been, honey?" he asked.

"Oh, who could talk business at a time like this?" she answered, her body undulating with practiced smoothness against Fargo's thighs and torso. "Let's go have some fun in my bed, you big devil, you."

Fargo already knew that business wasn't too good, because it was a spell until the monthly payday. When soldiers' funds ran short, they tended to go to the saloons instead of the cribs. It wasn't that they liked liquor better than sex, but taverns gave credit.

Fargo bent down to whisper to her. The way she licked and nibbled at his earlobe made it difficult to keep his mind on track, but he got the message across, and she agreed. It sounded like an easier way to earn twenty dollars than anything she'd done since turning professional a few years back on her fourteenth birthday.

Within minutes, they were riding double, her behind him and pressing against Fargo's back in a way that made him want to turn around and ignore their plans, when he finally heard the familiar shout of "Halt! Who goes there?"

"Fargo, the gent that brought in the camel. And I've got a guest."

The two sentries paused. One fumbled with some lucifers for a moment, and then Fargo was washed in the light of the bull's-eye lantern. He could see that both sentries were buck-toothed jug-eared kids that could have been brothers.

"Uh, Mr. Fargo," the one on the right said, "you can't bring her on the post. There's a rule about fancy gals."

"She ain't no fancy gal," Fargo insisted, dismounting and then helping the henna-haired woman down from the Ovaro. "Miss Laura Jones here was injured, and I was bringing her in to the post surgeon."

The hemming and hawing indicated that the sentries weren't about to believe Fargo, and Fargo really didn't blame them. The only thing he'd said that might even be close to the truth was that her name was Laura Jones, and Fargo rather doubted that that was the name she'd been born with.

But now the lantern light was playing on her blue silk kimono, stopping to focus on the way her erect nipples atop her full breasts swelled the thin material.

Fargo silently stepped sideways, circling in the darkness. "Honey," he said, "they won't believe us unless you show them where you're hurt."

With a flutter of hands, the kimono fell. The last thing the sentries noticed before getting knocked cold by Fargo's pistol butt was that Miss Jones was not a natural redhead.

Fargo felt sorry that their next stop was the stockade, rather than his room in the guest barracks, but this was one of those times when work had to come before play.

The adobe-walled stockade was easy to find, since it was one of the only buildings on the post where a lantern still glowed inside to ensure that no one would miss noticing that there were bars over the windows. Peeking through a front window, Fargo saw a skinny lieutenant sitting ramrod-straight at a meticulous desk. The shavetail was obviously fresh out of West Point; the only aspect of him that did not reek of spit and polish was his Adam's apple, which bobbed up and down like a berserk mine hoist every time he sipped tepid coffee from the shiny tin cup on his desk.

Fargo just stayed where he was, and motioned for Laura to knock smartly on the heavy pine door. The lieutenant marched over, asked some questions that were too muffled for Fargo to hear, and finally lifted the long bar and opened it because Laura sounded so distraught.

It was better to be a participant than part of the audience, Fargo thought as he observed that the lieutenant's back was slumping while another part was getting stiff and straight. Since they were across the room from his window, he couldn't hear much except that they were talking. From the look on the lieutenant's pimply face, he was having an awful time reconciling duty and orders with an opportunity to help a woman who was telling him that she wanted to file a complaint against a recently transferred Fort Union officer, a shameless scoundrel who hadn't kept his promises to her.

She looked ready to break into tears about this injustice. To comfort her, the lieutenant placed his arms around her. When they moved into a small side room that held a cot—to continue their discussion—and shut the door, Fargo moved inside. For whatever reasons, the shavetail had been too distracted to remember to bar the front door. Fargo paused to examine the logbook and to borrow a lantern before heading down the hall to the cells.

Normally, men in jail were as talkative as auctioneers, seeing as they didn't have much else to do. But these surly fellows just grunted when they saw Fargo holding a lamp in front of their tiny cell.

One was close to bald and sported an eye patch. The other seemed to have all the standard human equipment, although he resembled a ferret as he sat up from his cot and growled "What the fuck do you want?"

"I'll ask the questions around here," Fargo shot back.

"You law dogs never give up, do you?" the bald one grumped. "First one asshole with a badge, then another, and now one at night. We ain't got nothin' to say to none of you."

"Things might go easier for you if you told me who all was in on the Barclay Massacre," Fargo intoned.

"Do I look like a rat?" asked the hairy one with the long nose.

"Reckon not," Fargo agreed. "More like a weasel."

He pursed his lips and let loose a precise stream of tobacco-inspired spittle toward Fargo, who stepped back and checked his anger, sure that these hard cases knew a lot more than they were letting on about the troubles that the Ashford Trading Company had been experiencing on Santa Fe Trail. In the seething silence, he heard some noises up front and figured he'd best investigate.

"I'll come back. You'll be ready to talk then," Fargo announced, spinning on his heel.

"There'll be a blizzard in hell before we talk to you," the bald one snarled in parting as Fargo padded down the hall, lantern in one hand and drawn Colt in the other. Not wanting to charge in foolishly, he stopped at the door to the front room and listened for a bit.

"You . . . you . . . you painted harlot," the lieutenant was sputtering. That discovery shouldn't have come as any surprise to anyone who'd looked at Laura for more than ten seconds, and the lieutenant had been with her for a lot longer than that.

"That's shocking. That's disgusting. That's a crime against nature," the shavetail continued, his voice gaining some momentum before cracking again. "That's an abomination, what you said you wanted to do to my, to my, er, uh, manhood with your scarlet lips."

No wonder the damn country was in such trouble, Fargo thought, when the army let such idiots be officers. He heard the lieutenant say something about calling the MP's over Laura's shocking suggestion. Before the half-dressed man could get to the front door to holler, Fargo had come through the back door and caught the officer behind the ear with his pistol butt. Now there were going to be three men reporting for duty with awful headaches tomorrow.

Laura was standing over at the door to the side room, looking sassy as hell and naked as a jaybird. She did saunter over to help Fargo with the lieutenant, but watching her bend and breathe was pure distraction.

"Later," he said as much to himself as to her. "First we've got to get out of here, and we're going to have some company."

Fargo's pistol settled any arguments that the prisoners— Lem Sloat and Sid Hockett according to the logbook— might have offered about getting their hands tied behind their backs, having gags stuffed in their mouths, and being frog-marched outside, down to the stable while Laura pulled her kimono back on and kept the light going in the stockade office.

They didn't seem at all happy about being roped together and tied behind the mule, but Fargo really didn't care what they thought. He was leaving Fort Union tonight. He'd ridden in this afternoon with a warm-natured woman and a foul-tempered, spitting camel. He'd ride out with another warm-natured woman and some foul-tempered, spitting men.

Fargo suspicioned that if Colonel Canby was as worried as he let on about Indians on the warpath, the commanding officer probably wouldn't do much more than go through the motions about the escape from the stockade. Slipping away from indifferent soldiers would be a hell of a lot easier than hiding from eager Comanches.

It was too bad, Fargo thought, that he didn't know where they'd staked out the camel, or he could have sent it through the military herd, to see if army stock was any better behaved than Comanche ponies. Just to be safe, he lit the lantern once more and heaved it atop an empty shed that sort of stood by itself toward the edge of the fort. Making sure the rest of the tinder-dry buildings didn't burn down would likely keep the soldiers too busy tonight to pursue him.

And Fargo needed to buy all the time he could, because he wasn't going to make any speed as they headed into the rough ground that started a mile or two west of the fort. He and Laura were riding double, her in front this time. Behind them trailed the pack mule, which for once seemed to enjoy working as it pulled and kept Sloat and Hockett in step.

Several convoluted canyons twisted through these hills, and Fargo wasn't too particular about which one they might end up in by morning, when he would see whether Sloat and Hockett had changed their minds about talking to him.

Meanwhile, his attention drifted to other matters, primarily how nice Laura's sleek bottom felt when it bounced against his crotch with every step the Ovaro took. She leaned back against him, the front of her kimono falling open to the warm night, and Fargo's free hand found a most pleasing spot to rest.

When she whispered something to Fargo, he wasn't at all like that lieutenant. He didn't find this suggestion shocking. In fact, it sounded kind of sensible, considering. He stood in the stirrups for a moment while she twisted around to undo the buttons of his fly.

Then Laura went back to facing forward, arching that magnificent rump up while gripping the flanks of the saddle with her knees, and Fargo leaned back against the high cantle of his custom-made saddle. Before settling back, she hoisted her kimono and grabbed the horn, guided to Fargo's horn by his grip on her padded pelvic bones.

Fargo wasn't in a position to do much thrusting, but the Ovaro and the vagaries of this rocky trail took care of that for him as Laura settled back.

"My God," she gasped as she slid partway down Fargo's pole, "you mean there's more?"

Bounce by bounce, she took him in as she issued satisfied low moans, eventually grabbing the saddle horn to give herself more leverage for pushing back against Fargo. He wasn't keeping track of distance all that much, but they probably made at least two miles before he fired his first rounds.

Laura seemed pleasantly surprised that Fargo was still

ready for more after that, and mentioned that she'd like to turn around to try it again.

Fargo couldn't really object, although he wasn't too sure how it might work. But it wasn't as though they had much else to do except experiment as the Ovaro, mule, and prisoners plodded higher into the mountains.

Laura slid up and off. Still grasping the saddle horn, she bent her right leg and brought it across the saddle, holding herself up with her left knee as she pivoted, grasping Fargo's torso.

He had to sidle forward some and lean back farther than was really comfortable as she put her knees atop his thighs and then settled down, this time ready to start deep and fast all at once.

"The poor prisoners," she whispered in Fargo's ear between licks and nibbles. "Are we putting on a show for them?" Fargo hadn't thought to plug the prisoners' eyes and ears, so they likely had more reasons to be mad at him by now, but he didn't much care how much they detested him. And besides, it was mighty dark out.

"Never mind them," Fargo whispered back. "They told me they were closemouthed sorts, so they aren't likely to gossip about us."

She seemed to think that was funny and giggled some before settling down to some hot and luscious screwing, twisting and squeezing Fargo's throbbing shaft. When he bothered to think about it, Fargo knew that there were more comfortable ways to sit on a horse than with your knees jammed forward and your butt too far to the front while leaning back so much that the cantle was pounding your kidneys. But then again, there were damn few other ways that were as much fun.

They kept that up for three or four miles, until there was enough dim light in the sky for Fargo to look up and see that they were deep in a narrow canyon, the blue-gray sky just a jagged slit above them, framed by a craggy darkness.

As a professional lady who worked evenings, Laura kept different hours than most folks, which undoubtedly explained why she felt so chipper when the Ovaro halted next to a spring-fed pool.

The prisoners had hate-filled eyes as big as saucers, and Fargo just let them glare at him as he helped Laura down. They did stare a little harder after her bare feet found the ground and she stood facing them while nonchalantly buttoning the kimono before going down to the pond with Fargo.

The cold, sweet water was a relief on Fargo's parched throat. After they took their fill, he led the Ovaro down, then the mule. Laura went over and sat down on a convenient rock in the lush grass that filled the rest of this wide spot.

Fargo untied one prisoner at a time from the mule and marched the stumbling man over to the pond, holding his pistol behind the man's head as he undid the gag. Both times, he explained slowly that since the man hadn't wanted to talk earlier tonight, he wasn't going to say so much as a word now, or he'd get his head blown off.

Thus Lem and Sid opened their mouths only to drink. They did look a little peaked, so Fargo hiked them around the next bend, where there was a spot of bunchgrass and some shade from a scraggly mountain maple. Tying their lead rope to the maple, he told them he planned on sleeping for a while, and they were welcome to do the same thing.

That actually had been Fargo's intention, but Laura was splashing around, taking a bath when he returned, and she invited him on in. The water felt damn good when he joined her.

But since the pool wasn't all that deep, especially along one sandy edge where Fargo lay back and enjoyed the water lapping at his chest, Laura had another idea that ended up making him feel even better.

Her hand was already massaging Fargo's shaft into a vigor that surprised them both when she explained that a working girl deserved a hearty breakfast after a busy night.

Getting on all fours, she crawfished down a bit and bent her head down, her lips forming a small circle of flickering pleasure at the very tip of Fargo's organ. Her head moved down slowly, although her velvet tongue was in constant motion, rolling around the tip, then ever farther. And farther. And farther, until Fargo felt fit to explode, that if she ever came up for air, he'd punch a hole in the sky.

But her lips just kept moving down and her skilled tongue never let up until Fargo felt a surge that utterly drained him. Exhausted, he fell asleep where he lay, nestled against Laura, who turned around and pressed next to him in the sand and water.

6

The one trouble with these pleasant little canyons that wound through the foothills, Fargo thought as he woke with the sun's heat scorching his face, was that they turned into ovens every summer afternoon. Pulling himself up from the sand and ankle-deep water, he felt more warmth radiating from the variegated rocks that lined the deep cleft. Aside from the buzzing of insects and the insignificant noises Laura made while smoking a hand-rolled cigarette as she leaned against a poolside cottonwood, the place was silent.

She saw that he was awake, greeted him, and beckoned.

"I sure hope today turns out to be as much fun as last night." She smiled, batting her fake eyelashes, which looked out of place now that she'd washed the paint and powder off a face that really didn't need all that help to be attractive.

Fargo grinned and knelt next to her. "Hard to improve on, honey, but I wouldn't mind trying. Wouldn't mind it at all. First off, though, I better see if our baggage feels more talkative today."

She let loose a throaty laugh before a worried look settled on her face. "If I'd known we were coming up here, I think I'd have brought something besides this kimono."

"What you've got under it suits me just fine," Fargo consoled. "And we'll figure something out. This wasn't exactly in the plans when we rode into Fort Union last night." He rose, checked the horse and mule, and rounded the granite rib that separated the pool from the maple where Lem Sloat and Sid Hockett were tethered.

He had no idea which was which, so that seemed as good as any way to start after he prodded the prone men with his boot and they sat up, shaking their heads. A rest apparently hadn't improved their surly dispositions, judging by the way they glared at him.

He couldn't blame them for feeling proddy, the way that their hands were tied tightly behind their backs. Their legs were hobbled, too, a short rope connecting each man's restraints. A hemp rope connected their manacles to the tree, about fifteen feet away. And the gags couldn't have been very comfortable, either.

Ordering them to stand, he stepped behind them and untied their gags. The first sounds out were the raspy moans that could be expected from thirsty men, but by the time Fargo was facing them, the bald husky one with the eye patch was coherent.

"You fuckin' law dog."

Fargo just smiled and turned his attention to the other, whose ferret face was still twitching. The shorter man, so skinny that Fargo could make out his ribs under the man's sweat-soaked rough cotton shirt, managed to stammer that he didn't think too much of the way they'd been treated, either.

"To save some time, gents, I'm not a lawman. Name's Skye Fargo, and I aim to find out a few things today. Now which one of you is Lem Sloat, and which one Sid Hockett?"

Baldy was Sloat, it turned out. Upon hearing Fargo's name, Hockett's lean face looked even more weasellike. "You the one they calls the Trailsman?"

"Go to the head of the class." Fargo nodded. "Now, you boys feel up to talking, today, or are we going for another walk?"

"You son of a bitch," Sloat grunted. "Make us walk behind a skittish mule thinkin' we was gonna get dragged to death if it gets excited, and all the while you up there havin' your pleasure with that slut—"

The back of Fargo's hand caught him hard in the teeth, and Skye waited for the man to quit coughing. "I sure hope I misheard you there, Sloat. Best you understand that any woman I'm with is a lady, as far as anyone else is concerned."

Both nodded without enthusiasm.

"Glad we understand each other," Fargo continued. "Now you boys, along with a couple dozen other owlhoots, drifters, hard cases, and suchlike, have been hanging out up in Cimarron at Swink's Saloon lately, right?"

Something must have been quite interesting about the way their boots shuffled in the dirt, for they became intent on looking that way instead of at Fargo.

"I can tie you boys right over under that tree, where you'll have some shade," Fargo said. "And I can twist you some and tie your heads for you so that you'll have to look at me when we're talking. Or you can do it on your own. Entirely up to you."

Their sullen heads lifted. "Jesus, Mr. Fargo, we're thirsty. And I've gotta piss," Hockett rasped.

"Not my pants you've got on, so it won't bother me one bit if you piss right where you're standing," Fargo answered. "And I'll treat you boys to a drink just as soon as we finish talking."

Hockett scrunched himself up for a minute before the front of his ragged denim trousers began to moisten. Rather than watch, Fargo turned back to Sloat.

"The way I read it, you fellows decided to pester a wagon train between Wagon Mound and the Canadian a little more than a week ago. You rode down from Cimarron, and rode right into the train, acting friendly. Then you shot hell out of everybody, packed off such goods as you thought you could sell, and likely dug a pit and cached the rest nearby. Then you went home and rested up after a hard day's work."

Sloat started to say something and had second thoughts. He swallowed his words and resumed casting hatred that felt as intense as the sunshine. Hockett nodded.

"Now," Fargo continued, "there's God's plenty of wagon trains out there for the taking if you can ride in there friendly before you start shooting and stealing. I counted four or five myself coming up from Santa Fe. So I'd like you to tell me just why you picked the Ashford Trading

Company's train. For you see, Hank Barclay was a friend of mine."

Sloat winced, the furrows rising from his brow right on up his smooth skull, which was starting to redden from sunburn. "It was Vicente," Hockett interjected, "he told us that was the one to hit. We even got paid for it."

Even with the hobbles, Sloat could move his feet with blinding speed. He lurched forward with a spring, so that the rope connecting the two men's hobbles tightened and then pulled Hockett's feet out from under him.

The slender man went down sprawling. Then Sloat kicked his feet up again, so that he fell back, landing butt-first atop Hockett's lean rib cage. Fargo heard something crack, then some coughs, before he pulled out his Colt and told Sloat to stand up, slow and careful.

The way that Hockett was coughing up frothy blood, it was more than obvious that Sloat's forceful landing had shattered some ribs and shoved the jagged ends into the man's lungs. Still attached to Sloat as he rattled and rasped, he had maybe fifteen minutes to live. But he wouldn't be talking, at least not so anyone on earth could understand him, during that time.

Sloat just stood there impassively while his companion writhed at his feet, bubbles of spittle and blood emerging from his gaping mouth to pop and run down his cheeks, forming little balls of mud when they hit the ground. Sloat had taken his chances when trying to shut Hockett up in the only way available to him, but he'd succeeded. Hockett's beady brown eyes were now glazed, so Fargo knew that shock had set in. As agonized as Hockett looked, he wasn't in pain.

"Not bad," Fargo told Sloat, "not bad at all. Vicente Espinoza will doubtless admire your loyalty whenever I get around to telling him about this."

Sloat made spitting efforts without bringing anything up. "We finished talkin'?"

"Likely not," Fargo answered as Hockett's battered chest quit heaving. "I'd like to know just how close you boys were working with the Comancheros on that herd of mules you all stole last fall. And it would please me even more if you felt like explaining whether it was your crew

111

or somebody else that plundered a warehouse in Santa Fe last November."

Fargo was firing blind shots with his talk, looking for some confirmation to his suspicion that all the raids on the Ashbrook Trading Company had been related, that by tracking down one gang of outlaws and somehow ending their careers, he'd earn his ample pay from Cyrus Ashbrook.

But if Sloat held any answers, neither his face nor his voice betrayed such knowledge. Fargo wondered why the man had gone up the owlhoot trail when that aggression, stoicism, and ability to remain expressionless would have made him a wealthy legend at the poker tables of the West.

"Not my doing," was all Sloat said in his gravelly voice. His eye was flickering, though, its pale-blue iris rolling back and forth and up and down amid the bright-red veins, as if he were straining to look for something.

Fargo exhaled slowly. Sloat was a tough one, as tough as they came. With arms and legs tied, he'd just killed a companion to keep the man from talking. Which told Fargo that Sloat knew plenty that he wasn't telling. But how to get the man to talk? Fargo didn't have the stomach for torture, and even if he had, there was no guarantee that pain, no matter how intense, would make Sloat talk. Nor would the threat of death, for Sloat obviously knew that dead men tell no tales, and Fargo wanted to hear the story. But there was sure as hell no sense in making Sloat any more comfortable then he had to be.

"There may come a time, Lem Sloat," Fargo said slowly, "when you're going to wish that your buddy there could do for you what you just did for him."

Sloat's head and eye fixed on Fargo.

"That's right. You just might wish you were dead, and nobody around is going to be kind enough to kill you." Fargo waited for the words to sink in before continuing. "But for now, I'll make sure you get watered. Maybe even fed. You'll need your strength."

Sloat didn't even nod, just went back to twitching his eye.

Back around the granite rib, Laura had scrounged some

dead limbs from the scraggly piñon and juniper that dotted the less precipitous parts of the canyon wall, and had them heaped where she'd rolled some rocks together to form a fire pit.

Her ample breasts bouncing pleasantly beneath the sheer silk kimono, she dropped an armload of wood and ran over to embrace Fargo. "Skye, I sure hope we're staying here for a while. Or else we're going back."

"Why's that?"

"Because I'm really not dressed for travel. And all my other clothes are at my room."

Her royal-blue kimono did look worse for the wear. Sticks and branches had sharp spots that grabbed and tore the silk when she gathered firewood, and she didn't have any shoes. Doubtless she had a few outfits in her room by Fort Union, but there had to be some way around the problems that such a trip would cause.

"Can you sew?" Fargo asked.

She laughed. "I know how to do the things every woman knows how to do, you idiot. Maybe I'm not a great cook, but I can manage. Maybe I'd starve to death if I had to earn my keep as a seamstress, but I've always done my own mending. But I'm better than most at some, er, feminine talents, so that's how I earn my living."

"You won't hear me argue," Fargo agreed, fishing through his gear for the sewing kit he always carried for repairs while traveling.

The process of wearing Sloat down started with making him strip the clothes off the slender body of Sid Hockett. Wrinkling her turned-up nose, Laura obviously wasn't all that partial to the idea of washing the dead man's shirt and pants, then altering them to fit herself.

But Fargo was grateful that the woman wasn't horrified by the idea, either. While she tended to that, Fargo fetched a folding shovel from the possibles he'd packed on the mule, and put the surly and silent Sloat to work digging a grave in the rocky and shallow soil of the canyon bottom.

Leaning against the stubby spur of granite, Fargo could hear Laura's furious efforts to scrub Hockett's clothes while watching Sloat as he worked the short-handled shovel. The hobbled man moved slowly and deliberately in the broiling heat, but he was working. His blue eyes mere slits under his broad-brimmed hat, Fargo studied on what to do next.

It was almost a certainty that the infamous Vicente Espinoza had assembled some hard cases and drifters into a loosely organized gang operating out of Cimarron. Fargo's path had crossed Espinoza's two or three times, and Fargo knew it was dangerous to underestimate Espinoza, a mistake people often made. Fargo had almost made it himself a few years back, but had noticed the energy flashing in the short man's brown eyes. He had ended up sharing several bottles of fiery mescal with the outlaw, and when they parted, if they weren't exactly friends, they weren't enemies at the time, either.

Clad in his serape, sombrero, and sandals, Espinoza could pass for the most shiftless and lazy of Mexicans, almost comical to those white folks he encountered who were foolish enough to believe that all Mexicans were like that.

But Espinoza was more than good with a gun or knife, and he was a man with a grudge who could persuade other men to share his resentment. The way he saw it, he and his family had been happy, peaceful folk, who got by by growing corn, beans, and squash on a small plot watered by a community ditch, maintained every year by all the men in the neighborhood. They ran some livestock, too, a few sheep and goats, which ran on the common land, where everybody got their firewood, too.

Then came the Mexican War and the United States Army. Although there were all kinds of promises afterward that the old patterns of land ownership would be respected, the notion of common land, open to the community for grazing and the like, was totally alien to Americans. As far as the men who wrote the laws in Washington were concerned, land couldn't belong to everybody. It had to belong to somebody.

So Uncle Sam took title to land that had belonged to everybody in the neighborhood. And if it was federal land, it was open to all comers. Anglos moved in to cut its timber, to graze its ranges, to stake out homesteads, to take its water. People whose families had been hunting venison and firewood there for centuries were informed, in a harsh-sounding language they didn't understand, that they were now trespassers. They were run off at gunpoint.

And they got pissed off about it, as anybody would. Espinoza had decided that since the Americans had stolen from him, he'd return the favor. So Vicente had become one of the western outlets for the Comanchero.

The Comanchero were a motley collection of half-breeds and ambitious Pueblos, the only folk the Comanches would do business with, business that involved the cattle they regularly plundered from vast Texas herds.

The Comanchero swapped the Comanche stolen guns, ammunition, liquor, and other supplies for the stolen cattle, which were then moved west and sold along the foot of the Rockies, generally to the government for supplying military posts or reservation Indians. That irony was not lost on Espinoza, who took particular joy in collecting money from the hated U.S. government for cattle stolen in Texas.

But Hockett's last words were disturbing. They meant that Espinoza wasn't just in the general theft-and-trading business anymore. He was hiring out. Hiring out not just to steal from wagon trains, which was bad enough but understandable, but to butcher along the trail. It was frustrating as hell to know the who, but not the why. Sloat wasn't talking, and Fargo didn't figure that he'd get another chance to split a friendly bottle with Vicente Espinoza.

Sloat was waving to get his attention now, so Fargo straightened, flexed his back, and walked over, drawing his Colt just in case the silent and deadly man decided to use the shovel for a weapon.

The grave was a yard deep, no more, and just big enough to hold Hockett. "Looks good enough, Sloat," Fargo said, wincing when he saw the peeling blisters on the man's bright-red sunburned scalp. "While you bury him, I'll get you some food and water."

For a man who had to want food and water more than

anything else on earth, Sloat seemed totally unconcerned. He just nodded, put the shovel down, and dragged the naked corpse to the edge of the hole before standing and rolling the body in with his boots.

The late Sid Hockett's work shirt and denim pants looked a damn sight better on Laura than they ever had on him. She'd hemmed the trousers up and taken in the shirt a tad, although she was still barefoot, walking gingerly about their camp.

But the main reason the clothes looked so much better was that they were still damp and tended to cling to her rounded form.

Laura had a pot of stew going, made with some canned goods Fargo had packed on the mule and a few fresh greens she'd collected. She mentioned that some fresh meat would doubtless improve it, mayhaps a cottontail if Fargo'd be so kind as to get one.

"In another hour, that shouldn't be much of a problem," Fargo said, examining the sky. The sun was still blistering, but it wasn't far above the wall of mountains to the west. Once the shadows took over the canyon, sharp-eyed hawks and hungry coyotes would have a harder time spotting their prey, and the rabbits and other small critters would venture out of their burrows.

She nodded. "I'm in no hurry. Did Sloat tell you anything?"

"Nary a word," Fargo replied. "Maybe I'll wear him down and maybe I won't. I'm not going to make him comfortable, but I don't aim to torture him either." He picked up a canteen of stale, tepid water and a few sticks of jerky and stepped around the rock. Sloat had finished refilling the grave, so Fargo took the shovel, noticing that Sloat had poked at his tie rope with the dull blade.

But not enough to matter, Fargo judged. He tied Sloat's hands behind his back again and laid the shovel flat on the ground. Its business end was cupped just enough to hold some water, which Fargo poured into it, laying the jerky next to it in the dirt. Sloat would have to crawl on his belly like a snake to eat or drink, but the necessities were there. If he wanted to use them, that was up to him. Fargo knew there was more pleasant company nearby, so he didn't stay around to watch.

While the stew simmered and Fargo waited for some shadows for his rabbit hunt, he and Laura found some shade and seats under the cottonwood.

"Skye Fargo," she finally said after getting cuddled up comfortable next to him, "this all started last night as something real simple. You wanted me to distract some soldiers so you could talk to some prisoners in the Fort Union stockade. Being a working gal that sells various kinds of services, I took you up on it. If I remember right, the deal was that you'd bring me back to my quarters once all was said and done."

Fargo nodded and moved his arm down so his hand could console her firm right breast through the thin, rough cloth.

"So here I am," she continued, "up in the mountains somewhere with you and that Lem Sloat, with no idea what happens next. Do you mind telling me, or are you going to be as tight-mouthed as he is?"

Fargo had been worried that she might ask something like that. He had an answer, but he doubted she'd much care for it. The soldiers down at Fort Union now had every reason to complicate the hell out of Fargo's life if he went back down that way. So going on up into the mountains was the only reasonable course.

Since they'd ridden in at night, he wasn't sure which of several canyons this was, but he knew they all led west, where there was a trail that extended north and south along the flank of the Sangres. If they went south, they'd come across Glorieta Pass sooner or later, with a choice of going west to Santa Fe or east to Las Vegas. Going north on the mountain trail, they could strike Palo Flechado Pass and then go west to Taos or east to Cimarron, where the answers probably lurked under the tattered sombrero of Vicente Espinoza.

Either way meant traversing a lot of rough country, though, with a woman who was a lot more at home in a four-poster bed. But it wasn't like he had any need to keep secrets from Laura, so he explained the situation to her and asked what she thought.

"I wish you'd have asked me last night, when I had a choice," she murmured as her thigh pressed against Fargo's. "But it looks like we're pretty well stuck together for a while." She sighed. "Guess I could use a vacation, anyway, as long as you don't mind if I practice a little at my trade, just to keep from getting rusty."

Moving her hands to his shoulders, Laura began to roll atop Fargo, whose hands were already sliding under her drying shirt. But then she screamed and sprung. She didn't even slow down as her body crossed his and kept on going. Fargo glanced where she had been and realized that the coiled diamondback rattlesnake, thwarted by her lunge, was getting ready to strike him.

Maybe it would rattle first, the way that gentlemanly snakes were supposed to give warning, and maybe it wouldn't. In a race with the fangs, Fargo's right arm shot out and he seized the rattles at the tail end of the snake. With a snap of elbow and wrist, he swung the snake like a bullwhip in an arc that stretched to its full length, better than a yard, before its head smashed into one of the many rough rocks that littered their campsite.

While the rattler went through its death throes, wriggling its last, and Laura recovered her composure a few yards away, Fargo felt grateful that the rock had been so convenient. But there were lots of such rocks, in sizes from a man's head to too big to move, scattered about the narrow canyon floor, and their edges were all still relatively sharp and unweathered. Since the rocks were different than those of the canyon walls, Fargo knew they'd been carried down by water.

But this canyon, aside from a few spring-fed pools like the one they sat by, was dry. No doubt it carried a trickle in the spring, but certainly not enough of a flow to be moving anything bigger than pebbles. Besides, rocks carried down by water tended to get rounded, unless they'd been brought down from the higher country by a powerful current that didn't run very often—a flash flood. And the clouds upstream to the west were too dark and brooding for Fargo to feel quite comfortable.

Fargo returned his attention to the present, rather than what might happen, when he saw that the rattler's body was now convinced that the head was dead, and had quit writhing.

"I won't have to get a rabbit for the stew," he told Laura as she returned to his side, still breathing funny from her scare.

"You can eat snake?" she asked, wide-eyed. "It won't poison you?"

"Might as well put it to some use," Fargo replied, pulling out his knife. "Snake meat can taste kind of greasy sometimes, but generally it's pretty good. The poison's all up in some little sacks in the head."

Laura turned her eyes while Fargo skinned and cleaned the reptile, but she thought their sunset dinner was good enough to eat. Afterward, as they lay back atop his bedroll and wondered when the first stars would appear in the darkening sky, she mentioned that since she'd already had one snake in her mouth that afternoon, she felt inspired, and started fiddling with the buttons on his fly.

Undoing her trousers, Fargo was ready to give as good as he got, but he'd no more than started enjoying the supple smoothness of her when there was nearby thunder without lightning. Even worse for this evening's pleasures, he heard the piercing whine of a ricochet, just on the other side of that gray granite rib that had done such a good job of keeping Lem Sloat from looking on.

Laura responded to Fargo's sudden tensing, pulling back and away. Trying to reassemble his own clothes, he sat up, cursing, and scanned the rim of the canyon, silhouetted against the darkening sky. He could just barely make out a puffball of powder smoke to the west, floating listlessly in the gloaming.

Somebody up there obviously didn't like them, and before Fargo could think much more about it, there was a distant sparklike powder flash against the canyon rim, followed about a second later by the gun's roar, and then the whine of lead bouncing from rock to rock just around the bend. Another ball of smoke floated into the sky.

Laura didn't have any trouble deciding that the safest place, providing that the ambusher stayed up-canyon, was against their dividing wall. Fargo didn't reckon he'd learn any more by staying where he could see the shots, since that meant the shooter might see him, so he arrived next to her moments after she'd scuttled over there.

"Life sure never gets boring around you, Skye," she confided. "Short, maybe, but never dull."

"It's not over yet," he replied. "Just who the hell might that be up there shooting down at Sloat? Whoever he is, he's about out of light."

Her low voice was barely above a whisper. "There was talk all over Fort Union that whatever gang Sloat and that other man rode with was going to get them out before there was a trial or anything."

Before Fargo could answer, the distant gun belched again. They could hear the whistling slug strike the other side of the granite slab and then bounce away, howling into the gathering darkness. From the sounds, Fargo was sure it was a long-barreled Sharps buffalo gun, much like his own, and he thought momentarily about the target somewhere over on the other side of the rock, where the bullets were coming.

But under these circumstances, there wasn't much Fargo could do for Lem Sloat, even if he'd wanted to, so he looked back at Laura.

"That'd take some balls," he said thoughtfully, "to ride up against an army fort to bust two men out of the stockade."

"We did it," she said, and paused to clutch his torso as they crouched a little lower.

That might explain why there was at least one man up there with a gun. Vicente Espinoza's men might well have ridden up to Fort Union to fetch their *compadres*. For all Fargo knew, somebody from the gang could have done it legitimately by posting bond or something. But anyway, the gang could have discovered that Sloat and Hockett were gone, and followed the tracks up the canyon, then worked up to the rim.

Fargo realized ruefully that by sleeping through most of the day, along with various other distractions, he wouldn't have noticed much of anything up there, providing that there had been anything to notice.

But then, why would the gang be shooting at one of

their own, Sloat, whose bald head and eye patch made him recognizable even in the distance and near darkness? To shut him up, Fargo answered in his mental dialogue. Those guys did seem to put a premium on not telling anybody anything about what they were up to. And Sloat had been acting all day as if someone were going to rescue him at any moment, the way he was always casting around with that eye.

But then again, it was just as possible that the ambusher and his friends, if he had any, had merely happened along from above and just felt inclined to shoot at whatever they saw below. There were Jicarilla Apache hereabouts who might want to discourage white visitors to these mountains, although rimrock bushwacking wasn't generally their style. They preferred to sneak up closer, a lot closer. But one brave might have acquired a Sharps and started ambushing like a white man.

Some more rumbles made Fargo tense, until he realized that they were too distant and prolonged to be gunfire. And it was too dark now for the sharpshooter to be much of a menace.

Fargo edged over and stuck his head around the corner. "Hey, Sloat, you still in one piece?"

There was a grunt, which sounded healthy enough. Fargo wasn't inclined to check further, and even if he had been, noises down canyon grabbed his attention. The sounds were muffled echoes, not distinct at all, and the more he tried to concentrate on them, the more he felt Laura's heartbeat pressing against him.

That high-pitched sound that bounced around so much on the canyon walls, what could it be? Only one thing, Fargo decided, wishing he could talk himself into believing it was something else. But nothing seemed realistic except that it was a bugle, sounding the dismount call for the cavalry, who were no doubt stopping for the night down canyon about four miles, where the country was still reasonably open and there was another pool of good water.

But in the morning, they'd resume their pursuit of Fargo. They'd taken their time about coming, but they were coming. Staying the night where they were suddenly made no sense at all, even if it hadn't been for the bushwhacker up on the rim.

Staying here or heading back down meant riding right into the arms of the soldiers. If they didn't shoot him on sight, Fargo had a good chance of growing old in the stockade. They'd charge him with destroying government property, arson, disruption of a military command, assault on an officer, abetting the escape of prisoners—probably everything except leprosy.

On up the canyon trail? They wouldn't make time worth mention, going into an inky night riding double, trailing a mule and a man on foot. Not to mention that there was no way to do that quietly, and the ambusher, should he still be up there, could get lucky with a sound shot. Given the choices, though, that direction was obvious.

"If you've got any better ideas, I'll be glad to listen," he told Laura, "but it strikes me that we'd best pack up and head up the canyon."

She agreed, and they scurried about the campsite, stumbling some in the darkness. The last embers of the campfire provided a little light, but they didn't dare stoke it with fresh wood for fear that they would then be too visible to the man on the cliffside, if he were still there.

They were packed up, except for Sloat, and Fargo was going over to get him when he felt the ground vibrate. The Ovaro had been skittish, which he'd dismissed as mere annoyance at night travel. But there was moisture in the air and now came a low rumbling from the west, too low to be thunder.

Here he was in the dark with a barefoot woman and a shackled man mean enough to curdle milk in the cow, with the army coming after him from one way, a sniper waiting for him up above, and what had to be a roaring flash flood due within the hour, depending on just how the curves in this canyon might slow down the torrent's arrival. The only way left to go was down.

Fargo felt his way from the maple toward the end of Sloat's tether and jerked up on it. He could make out Sloat's rising bulk and wasted no time in clubbing the

head with his pistol. Fargo cut the rope and felt pleasantly surprised with his own strength as he shouldered the
two-hundred-pound man and got him over to the mule.

With another slash of the knife, the diamond hitch
he'd tied so painstakingly in the dark was but a memory,
and Fargo didn't feel too good about how he had to cut
off the straps that held the panniers aboard, either. But it
was a relief to lay Sloat down atop the saddle in the
bedroll's place, his belly wedged between the cross bucks
of the packsaddle. Fargo warned the mule not to get
frisky for a few moments, and managed to get Sloat's
hands and feet tied together somewhere under the mule's
belly.

"What're we doing, Skye?" Laura finally asked.

"We aren't doing anything for a while, honey," Fargo
answered, stressing the first word and hating what he was
going to say. "You are going to get on my Ovaro and
ride down toward the army, just as fast as he'll take you.
I am going to get up this damn canyon wall somehow."

She started to question him, but Fargo held her arms
and pulled her against him. "Listen, Laura, you don't
have much time. That rumble you hear and sometimes
feel is a flash flood on its way. You take the horse and
mule downstream toward the soldiers. It widens out down
there and you'll be able to ride up on a rise or something. That big pinto'll pull you through if the soldiers
don't. And the army won't have anything against you,
especially if you come back with one prisoner. Got that?"

He felt her head nod against his arm. "But what
about you?"

"I aim to get as high as I can in the half an hour or
whatever before the water gets here."

"Your horse?"

"If I'm alive enough to need him, I'll figure that out
later. But my chances with the water look better than my
chances against the army. It works the other way around
for you folks. Now, get!"

He helped her astride the saddle and patted both her
and the Ovaro for what he hoped wouldn't be the last
time. Now all he had to do was scramble up a sheer
cliffside in near total darkness.

Working more by feel than sight, Fargo found the edge of the familiar granite rib and grasped its sides, then straddled it and shinnied up a yard or two. He supposed that if a man really had to castrate himself, he'd pick an implement that gave less pain than this rock edge, which dug into his crotch with every agonizing move.

Half-wondering if he'd be singing soprano before breakfast, Fargo found that the rock's top, probably a dozen feet above the canyon floor, was broader, wide enough to crawl on. He made fairly good time for the next twenty feet, until the big slab joined the sheer canyon wall. Feeling around for handholds advised him that cactus would grow just about anywhere.

His grasping hands eventually struck something he could grab, something that had to be an outthrust root of one of the scraggly piñon that managed to grow in every spot that wasn't totally vertical. But it was far above him. Even on tiptoes, his belly to the wall and a prickly pear that didn't know any better than to grow there, Fargo could only get three fingers around the root, which sloped down anyway.

Trusting it might mean he'd slide off, or the damn thing could break. But that upstream roar was getting louder even as he wrestled for a better grip, so he put all the strength he could muster into getting higher, faster.

He tightened his arm and started pulling, clawing at the wall with his knees and feet and telling himself that the cactus didn't matter. He managed to get both hands full on the root, which was starting to feel queasy about his weight. A desperate scrambling lunge got his left hand to a more solid chunk of the tree, and moments later, he and the piñon were sharing a ledge that wasn't more than six inches wide, judging from the way he had to stand with his feet sideways to feel at all secure.

Staying calm from this perch was about as easy as sitting quietly on a hot stove, considering that the upstream roar now sounded like the middle of a buffalo stampede, but Fargo forced himself to settle down before resuming his exploration of the canyon wall. He could think of about two dozen things he'd done in the past couple days that he'd do differently now, if he'd known what was coming, but he told himself that a man could run into trouble no matter what he did or where he went. The trick was not to fret about how things might have gone different, but to use your wits and whatever was handy to overcome what the world threw at you.

Pushing his hands against the rock wall and wishing he had something to hold on to, Fargo shifted his feet gingerly until he felt the base of the piñon behind his boots. He lifted his right foot, knowing that there was a low branch somewhere over there that he could use for a step. This process would be much simpler if he could see what he was doing, but he wasn't sure he'd like what had to be a terrifying view, so things probably worked out about even.

There. He had his heel hooked over that branch, which wasn't as low as he remembered. Slowly extending his right leg, he pushed up while moving his stretched hands up the rock. Even a fingerhold would be an improvement over what he was finding, but eventually his left fingers found a ledge, one that felt fairly substantial. His right hand moved over as he gauged its width and probed back to see if it was deep enough to hold him.

So far, so good, Fargo told himself. His hands were now gripping a relatively secure place, and if he could work his feet farther up the tree, he'd be soon be able to perch easily on this rock ledge that he couldn't see.

His left boot heel had just hooked over a branch when hell came around the bend and roared into his section of canyon. Fargo couldn't see the wall of muddy, roiling water; even if there'd been light, he wouldn't have dared to turn around for the view. But he could feel it.

A surge of wet air, pressurized and pushed by the flood, pushed against Fargo's eardrums, momentarily overwhelming the tumult of the water. He ground his teeth, then forced a yawn, hoping the chewing motion would restore equilibrium to his eardrums before he lost his balance.

Fargo knew he'd managed, because his giddy feeling vanished and his hearing returned. The flood was coming any moment now, although its noisy front wall seemed to proceed more slowly than he'd anticipated. Even in the thundering uproar, he could make out distinct sound patterns. Rolling boulders thumping against the canyon wall, trees being ripped out of the narrow canyon floor, limbs and rocks crashing and grinding against one another, all of it magnified by the echoing of these steep rock walls that the torrent was struggling against.

Judging that the seething torrent was almost directly below him, and not at all sure that it would stay down there, Fargo prepared himself for a leap at the ledge. He launched himself and felt the once steady piñon melt as the noise reached a level that was almost painful. With every bit of energy he could muster, he pulled himself onto the ledge as the flood thundered by, perhaps a yard or two below, sweeping out his piñon with one swift crash in the dark.

This ledge seemed to run uphill from Fargo's perch, and he was of two minds. Going on up, if it was possible to do so while keeping his feet on something solid, made a lot of sense. Anything that took him away from that boiling roar just a few feet below his boots seemed mighty sensible.

But he couldn't see a damn thing. The footing was good where he stood, and the crest and the front of a flash flood were pretty much the same thing. The water might rise a foot or two in the next couple minutes, but after that, tonight's excitement would subside. Long before morning, the scoured canyon would hold only pools and trickles.

Fargo eased himself down and got as comfortable as he'd been for a while, leaning his back against the cliff while sitting with his legs dangling out above the flow, which was already settling down.

He tried to judge whether Laura would have been able to get out of the canyon in time. It was only three miles or so to open ground, which would dissipate the water's force. And the Ovaro had been in a hurry when he'd sent them off.

So Laura should have made it, he told himself, and the

soldiers had to be camped at least that far below, and likely even farther out into the flatter country. Bugle calls could be heard from a considerable distance.

Not that the Trailsman could do much about it, no matter what was happening down the canyon. He found enough room on the ledge for him to stretch flat on his back, and he felt small pebbles and ridges trying to bore into his spine and shoulders. But even at that, he didn't feel like looking for a better place to sleep tonight.

7

When the slowly brightening sky woke Fargo and reminded him how sore a man's back could get after a
night of sleeping on a bare rock ledge, he got to wishing
that some huge bird would happen by, so that he could
just hop aboard its back and sail away. That looked to be
the only reasonable way to get anywhere from where he
stood and stretched.

The scraggly piñon that had helped him reach this
perch was long gone, torn away by the vicious surge that
had scoured the canyon below. For as far as he could
see, the trees and grass had been replaced by bare,
jagged rocks and wet gravel. Looking straight down, he
noticed that the granite rib was still in place, and Sid
Hockett's grave was likely still where Sloat had dug it,
since tons of mud, boulders, cobbles, and the like had
piled up behind the protruding slab.

He had his Colt and knife, his clothes, and no way to
get down without wings. So he started up, sidling along
the ledge to where it narrowed to a couple of inches, less
than he felt comfortable trying to balance on. But there
the bare rocks were no longer smooth. Finding handholds and footholds amid the clefts and outcrops was
considerably easier when he had some light, and soon
Fargo was up to where the canyon wall was no longer so
steep as to require him to navigate on all fours. By the
time that sunrise was official, he was in the trees along
the rim, ponderosa that looked thick from afar but actually left quite a bit of room between their trunks.

The long shadows from the low light made tracks in

the sandy soil stand out like whores at a church social, so Fargo didn't have a bit of trouble finding the route of last night's ambusher. The man had ridden up fairly leisurely, stopping often to dismount and walk over where he could peer down into the canyon. At some point farther up, he'd spotted Sloat, but not Fargo and Laura on account of that granite rib, and had set up shop and started shooting.

When darkness made further sniping impossible, he'd headed back down, still taking his time. As Fargo followed the return tracks, he saw right where the rider had been when he and his mount heard the roar of the flash flood. The horseshoe prints instantly got deeper, but less distinct, because each hoofbeat was scooping out sand and pine needles, spraying the stuff behind it.

The trail rounded the brow of a foothill, giving Fargo a breathtaking view of the prairie rolling east toward the sun, its wavy surface broken by a few mesas, buttes, and isolated rises. At his feet the tracks were joined by others, and he studied on the impressions for a minute. Two other riders had come this far and waited, he decided, noticing their aimless, shuffling bootprints about the clearing.

Their friend the bushwhacker had returned, and they'd all continued on down. Since they'd probably taken the easiest route—being, as it was, dark and horses left to finding their own way seldom did any more work than they absolutely had to—Fargo just kept with the trail as it wound toward the flats, with Fort Union's flagpole visible. Old Glory waved among the bunchgrass and sand, and the distant strains of reveille joined the chirping of the jaybirds.

Their trail had neared bottom when Fargo saw signs of a commotion and tracks coming in from his left, up from the canyon outlet: tracks that he knew well—the caulked shoes he always specified for the Ovaro, and the slender U-shaped shoes that the mule had once tried to plant on his chest. Past the disturbed area, the tracks of four horses and a mule led north, where the sea of mud and flotsam left by last night's flood buried the trail.

Five minutes either way, and Laura would be back

home by now, with Sloat returning to the stockade, and maybe the army deciding it had something better to do than look for Fargo. But she'd escaped the flood, only to ride right into the ambusher and his two friends. It was safe to bet that her going on with them wasn't exactly her choice. Over on the other side of this morning's big mudhole, the tracks continued north, so likely she was now a captive of Espinoza's gang.

Espinoza had Fargo's horse, his mule, the woman he'd been with, his Sharps, such gear as the flood hadn't hauled away, and the explanation for the raids on Ashbrook. Fargo had his clothes and his Colt, and maybe two hours to walk before the sun got brutal, perhaps less than that if an early patrol from Fort Union happened upon him. He let loose a few oaths, which seemed to amuse the nearby prairie dogs before they scuttled into their holes, and worked his way downhill around the flood's residue.

It was small consolation to see tracks indicating that the pursuing soldiers had gotten out of their bivouac in time, and a pisser to think that the army was still after him rather than after Espinoza. He couldn't think of a thing in the world he could say to Colonel Canby that might keep him out of the stockade and put the soldiers to work doing something useful.

Once he'd left the area of the canyon mouth, Fargo headed north, tending west toward the foothills where there was cover and a better chance of water. There were some settlements, ranches and the like, within ten or fifteen miles, and if he kept moving, he might reach one before sundown. He topped yet another sandy rise and had to stop at what he saw below him.

It looked like a scene out of one of the Bible stories he'd heard when he was a kid. Down in the swale stood his recent four-legged acquaintance, the camel, except now there was a riding saddle across the animal's shoulders, and a packsaddle of sorts with panniers straddling the beast behind its hump.

A few feet off stood a small, swarthy, bearded man wearing a flowing pale robe and some cloth headgear that wrapped around his brow and trailed into a sort of canopy extending to his shoulders. As Fargo stood and watched, the man reached into his robe, pulled out a watch or compass and consulted it, then adjusted a blanket that he'd spread on the ground, and knelt on it, hands clasped before his bowed head.

When the man got up after his prayers, Fargo was standing right behind him, Colt in hand, and ready to add camel theft to the other reasons the army might be after him.

The man turned, his eyes growing wide at the sight of the revolver before he looked on up at Fargo's eyes, glowing blue under his wide-brimmed hat.

"Good morning," he finally said, his words clear through a guttural accent. "Why is your gun drawn?"

"I aim to borrow your camel," Fargo replied, "whether or not you cooperate."

"Unless you want him for meat, which is tough and stringy, he will not be of use to you," the robed man said seriously. "Camels will not kneel for just anyone and let people ride them."

Fargo recalled which of his grunts had worked best earlier, and hollered them at the beast. It turned its head and looked ready to spit, but then straightened its long neck and knelt.

"You must be the man I heard so much of at Fort Union," the amazed man exclaimed. "Fargo. The Trailsman. The American who rode in on the camel."

Fargo nodded. The man growled something at the camel to indicate that this had been a false alarm and he could get back up, and returned his attention to Fargo. "I am Sergeant Ahmet Muhammad of the Sixth Regiment of the Cavalry of His Excellency, Sultan Abdulmecid, may he live forever."

"And you ended up halfway around the world from your home in Turkey, tending camels for the Yankee army," Fargo answered, recalling that the Fort Union remount officer had said something about a getting a Turk to fetch the beast.

"Yes." the man smiled. "It sounded interesting, so I volunteered." Fargo was beginning to like the Turk, because the man maintained his composure even with the

Colt pointed right at his chest. "If you do not kill me, it is my job to take Alkazar down to Fillmore."

"Mind if I call you Ahmet?" Fargo asked.

"It is, what you say, okay? And you are called Fargo?"

"Well, Ahmet, it's like this." Fargo told his story, from the meeting with Ashbrook through the abduction of Laura last night. Judging by his deep laughter, Ahmet thought it was pretty funny the way he and Laura had diverted the army in order to see Sloat and Hockett.

"So you wish to use Alkazar to visit these bandits and rescue your woman and get them to tell you why they attacked your friend's caravan?" the Turk asked after Fargo was done.

The Trailsman nodded.

"I know you can ride Alkazar," Ahmet said, "but your trip sounds interesting. May I be part of it? It matters not to me if I am somewhat late in arriving at Fort Fillmore. After all, I am not really in your army."

Figuring the heathen Turk couldn't be any less trustworthy than other folks he'd met on the trail, Fargo holstered the Colt. "We can ride double?" he asked.

The Turk lowered his head, turned it, and spat before returning to face Fargo with a broad smile, his teeth shining against his swarthy complexion and full black beard. "Let me show you what we can do if we are not forced to ride with your stupid soldiers."

The camel saddle sat pretty much where Fargo had sat during his brief career as a camel driver, and Fargo was perched behind it as Ahmet urged the beast into a ground-eating lope that would have strained a horse mightily for any length of time. And Alkazar the camel kept it up for hours as they pounded northward across the rolling prairie at the base of the foothills.

Only once did they stop. Fargo sipped from the canteen, feeling a bit uncertain as to what he should be doing, while Ahmet repeated the ritual Fargo had seen earlier—stopping to consult his compass, then lay out a short blanket and pray.

Soon they were on their way again, generally following the trail of the Ovaro and the abductors. When they spotted a wagon train ahead, coming along down the mountain branch of the Santa Fe Trail, fresh from Cimarron, Fargo wished they weren't on a camel, so he could ride down and ask if they'd noticed anything unusual back in Cimarron, which couldn't be more than another ten miles. Aboard the camel, they'd already covered better than twenty miles this morning, and the ungainly mount didn't even seem winded.

But Ahmet steered his dromedary off the trail, up toward the piñon-spotted hills, and stopped for a while. While they munched on some jerky—the Turk said it was an improvement over his native trail foods, even if a mullah back home would have judged it unclean and thus an affront to Allah's notion of proper food—he asked Fargo what he planned to do once they caught up with Laura and her captors.

"Kind of depends on where we find them and what we've got for weapons, doesn't it?" Fargo replied.

"I like you, Fargo," the Turk answered, finally allowing himself a chance at the canteen. "Most of you Americans, you always have a plan. Plan, plan, plan. And plans never work right, do they?"

"Can't say that my own have been working real well lately," Fargo said. "We ought to be catching up to them pretty shortly, shouldn't we? They had a six- or eight-hour start or better on us, but that Alkazar can sure cover ground."

"We will be upon them soon," Ahmet agreed. "No horse stays ahead of a camel in open country." He paused, examining Fargo with his flashing eyes. "You have your Colt and your knife." He opened his flowing robe to reveal a brace of pistols, as well as a crisscross bandolier, all strapped on atop an inner robe.

One of Ahmet's canvas saddle boots held one of those newfangled Henry repeating rifles that the army was trying out these days, and the other carried a gleaming curved scimitar, longer than Fargo's arm and no doubt sharp enough to shave with. If they didn't have to do anything at long range, he and Ahmet were equipped to take on anything this side of the Comanche Nation.

After they remounted, they stuck to the edge of the foothills, just outside the trees, where they could see the

Mountain Branch off and on. Not that there was much down there, or in any other direction Fargo looked while locking his knees and gritting at the way the camel's spine worked against his butt. This trip was certainly faster than walking, but otherwise it wasn't much of an improvement.

Fargo spotted what had to be some familiar tracks ahead, coming up from below and to the right. Before he could holler at Ahmet to stop, the camel driver's sharp eyes caught the indentations. He reined up and scanned the ground. "Four horses and a mule, Fargo. They are your people?"

Little more than a mile up their trail toward the mountains, there was evidence of a short halt. At least one man had dismounted to take a leak; the ground was still damp, which meant they weren't more than thirty minutes ahead.

Fargo looked for another sign, hoping that Laura was getting better treatment than he'd given Sloat. But there wasn't any way to tell from what he could see here.

Ahmet grunted at Alkazar, and they resumed their swaying way up into the foothills as the sun set before them. The trees were starting to get thick in the twilight when Ahmet pulled up, the camel knelt, and they got off.

In open land, the camel had been swift and tireless. He still showed no sign of being winded, but Ahmet explained that camels didn't navigate very well at all in forests. They weren't nimble enough to turn quickly when there were trees and other obstructions, and a man sitting atop one was high enough to get whacked by limbs he wasn't expecting.

Fargo had been feeling kind of seasick and saddle sore anyway, so he didn't mind walking at all. The cool evening breeze in his face felt good enough to keep him from thinking too much about the chafed spots on his legs and butt, and he hadn't walked far, only enough to get his legs unkinked, when he smelled the spicy aroma of piñon smoke.

From their vantage in some deadfall, Fargo and Ahmet could make out their quarry's camp. Alkazar could likely make it out too, but he had his eyes shut and he looked like he was chewing, although he hadn't eaten anything all day. About a hundred yards off, a ways up from a hit-and-miss creek, four men were setting up for the night.

Sloat, easy to recognize on account of his eye patch, had acquired a hat; he was leering at Laura while pulling Fargo's saddle off the Ovaro. The way Laura was riding the mule was something of an improvement over the way he'd left Sloat there, since she got to sit up, but her bare feet were tied under it, and sitting in a packsaddle couldn't have been real comfortable. Fargo choked down a wave of rage and eyed the rest of the setup.

All three of the others looked mean, and good at it from the wary way they moved. They weren't kids out playing outlaw, but men who had managed to stay ahead of posses for years. Fargo recognized the scarred, lean face of Manuel Chico, a half-breed Comanche reputed to enjoy cutting up his victims, slowly, a piece at a time, for days.

The other two, even when they passed close to the fire that Chico was tending, had faces Fargo might have seen sometime, somewhere, but he had no names to attach to them.

The taller one was too bowlegged to bring his knees together on a bet, and so thin that calling him Slim would have been exaggerating. The other matched Sloat's general proportions, husky and wide-shouldered, but of average height. All the other men wore normal trail garb, but he fancied greasy buckskins with tattered fringes. Which was the way buffalo hunters tended to dress, which meant he'd probably been the fellow with the Sharps last night.

Laura sat impassively atop the mule, her hands tied to the front cross buck of the saddle, and when she turned, Fargo saw that she was gagged.

Once the horses were tended and tied to a line they'd stretched between trees, the camp settled down to some dinner—fried buffalo tongue from the smell of it. That is, two of the men sat down to eat.

The other two remained standing, just beyond the

fringe of dancing light from the fire, so shadowed that Fargo wouldn't have been able to spot them if he hadn't followed their motion.

They were damn good at riding the owlhoot trail, Fargo swore to himself. They'd have sentries up and about all night. After dinner, when they all decided to take their turns atop Laura, once they'd stripped her and tied her spread-eagled to the ground, one or two of them would keep his pants and pistol on to stand guard. They just weren't going to be as easy to distract as the soldiers had been.

"Do you want any of them left alive, besides the woman?" Ahmet whispered.

"I'd like to talk to one of them, and Sloat's not too talkative," Fargo whispered back.

The wind shifted so they could hear the campfire talk, and both men became instantly still as the faint sounds drifted toward them.

"Tell you, havin' to walk in the dirt while that Fargo asshole was a ridin' and a fuckin' at the same time kind of stuck in my craw," Sloat said to no one in particular. "So I reckon I get to have at her first tonight."

From the way Laura stiffened at that, Fargo could tell she was the only one who wasn't joining a murmured chorus of agreement, and he had a feeling that her objections amounted to more than just not being paid for her work.

"You fuckers sure had me scared for a while there," Sloat continued, now as talkative as he had been silent, "when Charlie started takin' potshots at the camp."

Charlie was the one in buckskins. "If I'd've been meanin' to hit you, you'd be dead. The idea was to get Fargo to stick his head out from behind that rock, so's I could blow it off. Goddamn Sharps just won't shoot through a rock wall, an' I don't see through 'em none too good, neither."

By straining his ears, Fargo could hear Chico and Slim, which might as well be his name, join in the chuckling at Charlie's statement.

But Sloat had been eager as hell to shut Sid Hockett up, permanent, when it looked as though Hockett might say anything about what Espinoza's crew was up to these days. Which meant that no one was eager for Sloat to talk, either. So not many tears would be shed if Charlie had hit Sloat. Not any more than if he'd hit Fargo.

The breeze shifted again, and their voices became just indistinct sounds as the conversation drifted to how narrowly they'd escaped the flash flood and speculation as to how dead Fargo had to be by now.

Ahmet tugged at Fargo's sleeve, and they retreated in silence, the camel following like a big quiet dog.

As Fargo saw it, the only advantage they might have was surprise. With his Sharps, he wouldn't have had much trouble taking down an outlaw or two from their distance. But a Henry wasn't good at that range. Getting closer meant sneaking up, through crackling brush and deadfall, on a camp guarded by men who were good at it, too good to take chances against if there was any other way.

The problem was that there didn't seem to be any other way. And even if that worked, a gunfight in a crowd meant lead flying every which way, which wouldn't improve Laura's health a damn bit.

Fargo did feel obligated to this Fort Union whore who loved adventure, and he felt mad as hell about some worthless shit like Lem Sloat riding his Ovaro. But he was about out of ideas when Ahmet whispered.

"Surprise no good, right? No sneaking on them."

Fargo muttered agreement, not liking how foul-tempered he felt, seeing another man with his horse and a lot of men eager to gang-rape a woman he liked, and being with a Turk who insisted on repeating the obvious.

"Can you make them look the other way? Toward the horses?"

"Reckon so," Fargo answered, thinking madly and then remembering the mule. "Got a short piece of chain?"

Ahmet rose and went over to pet the camel's head, then fished something out of the panniers. All Fargo could really see were shadows, cast by the dim light of the distant fire as well as tonight's sliver of a moon, shimmering in a star-filled sky.

The Turk returned, his hand finding Fargo's to press

about six inches of coiled, linked metal into his palm. It felt like a chain bit, one of those cruel things you stuck in horse's mouths sometimes when there wasn't any other way to convince them that you were in charge. No doubt it worked the same way on a camel, Fargo thought.

By the time that Fargo could swing halfway around the outlaw camp, moving more slowly than he wanted to, but knowing that he didn't dare make any noise, all the men had eaten and they were laughing about how well Laura was going to do for dessert.

That is, Charlie the buffalo hunter and Sloat were laughing as Charlie stood behind the trussed woman, holding her in place so that Sloat could grab each lapel of his late companion's shirt and rip it open, buttons popping off and dropping into the sand and pine needles of the clearing.

"My, my, look at them titties," he announced, stepping back a bit to enjoy the view of her heaving, full breasts, even firmer now because she had her back so stiffly arched. As his hands moved forward, she tried to spit toward him. It was just a gesture, since her mouth was still gagged.

Which didn't annoy Sloat at all. "I likes it when they fight and squirm some." He got his hand on each breast and pushed and rubbed.

Fargo crept forward. Slim had headed toward the other side of camp, and he knew Chico was somewhere on this side, likely not too far from the horses. Shifting to his left as he continued his stealthy movement toward camp, Fargo finally saw the horses outlined against the fire.

Over their backs, he could just see the heads of the trio by the fire—Sloat's bald dome, peeling with sunburn; Laura's shoulder-length curly red hair, twisting and bobbing, and Charlie, still wearing his greasy plainsman's hat.

Knowing he had to figure out where Chico was before he did much more, Fargo pulled a fist-sized rock out of the ground and heaved it to his right. It landed with a satisfying thud, causing some motion in the shadows up ahead, just to the left of the horses. The crouching Chico rose just enough for Fargo to make out the silhouette of his head.

Fargo crept on forward, straight toward the horses. He couldn't tell which was which, except for the one he was looking for, the mule. Its long ears made a V right in the middle of the row, with two horses on each side. None of the animals had stirred worth mention, which was understandable. They had to be at least four kinds of tired, considering the kind of hard travel they'd been through in the past two days.

Within a couple yards of the rear of the horses, Fargo tossed another rock to his right. Chico straightened again, then stepped along the front of the horses, his pistol drawn. When he got in front of the mule, Fargo rattled his chain.

Absolutely nothing happened, except that Chico was now frozen in position. Flat on the ground and looking at the world with a view framed by the mule's legs and belly, all Fargo could see was Chico's crouched torso, which blocked most of what was going on by the fire. From the way bare legs kicked out every now and again, Laura no longer had her pants on.

The only thing you can count on mules for, Fargo decided, was being contrary. When you didn't want them to kick and bite, they did. When having the thing get frisky was a matter of life and death, the damn thing was asleep, probably dreaming of some mulish paradise where there were no harnesses or halters and the men did all the heavy work when they weren't being kicked or bit by frolicking mules.

Fargo's edginess resulted in a snapping twig, which he rolled away from as soon as he felt it. Chico straightened and shot with deadly accuracy toward where the sound had come from. Having a .45 fired six inches from its long, sensitive ears awoke the mule. Fargo saw its legs twitch and tried another shake of the chain bit.

Now the mule was sure somebody was fixing to hurt it, and the nearest somebody was Chico. It reared back, then lashed out its front legs at the astonished bandit, raking his chest with its sharp hooves and steel shoes as he went to the ground. With a triumphant bray, it sprang forward, stomping on his thrashing legs.

Chico raised his gun's muzzle toward the approaching mule's muzzle, but the mule got its teeth on his wrist first and the shot went harmlessly into the air. Just for good measure, Fargo stood up and rattled the chain some more, then ran to his right, around the horses, toward camp.

He got there just in time to see Ahmet stroll into the clearing, ambling along like a man without a care in the world, as if he'd just stopped by to ask directions or something. Except that in his right hand was that shiny scimitar, a wicked curved blade at least two feet long, gleaming in the flicker of the campfire, except for the spots that were bloody. In his left hand, he held a shank of hair the casual way that women held shopping bags, but the hair was still attached to Slim's head, his eyes and mouth still gaping as blood dripped down from what had been his neck.

With the ruckus over by the horses, Charlie had let go of Laura and headed over that way, kneeling just out of range of the thrashing mule's hooves to try to pull Chico out. Sloat hadn't given up on Laura; he had her naked body pushed to the ground, although he hadn't finished taking his pants off. He looked up to see Slim's head staring at him, dangling from the Turk's hand.

Even through the gag, Fargo could hear Laura's scream of horror and she put every available muscle into a buck that would have done the mule proud. Sloat rolled off her and tried to crawfish away from the Turk, who swung Slim's head like a sling and loosed it into Sloat's head, the two skulls meeting with a thud.

Charlie, apparently figuring there wasn't much more he could do to keep the gasping, screaming Chico's chest from being stomped into jelly, started to his feet and reached for his own pistol, a notion Fargo discouraged with a shot to the shoulder that spun Charlie around twice during his collapse to the ground. Fargo wanted at least one of the men alive, but leaving men alive didn't seem to be one of Ahmet's major concerns.

Perhaps that wasn't quite right, Fargo conceded on his

way toward them, his steps slow as he tried to watch everything all at once.

The grinning Turk had paused to slit the rawhide manacles that bound Laura's wrists, his sword slicing a big arc so fast that it was a blur, yet so precise that only the leather was cut, even though her hands were tied closely together. With an elegant but casual thrust, he implanted the scimitar's tip in a chunk of firewood.

As it quivered there, he politely bowed and doffed his outer robe, presenting it to Laura, who was obviously too stunned and frightened to care what she might be wearing.

A few paces away, Sloat got up on all fours, crawling toward the woods. Charlie, over toward the other side of the clearing, had given up on lying there to bleed to death, and was trying to sit up, holding his pistol before him with both shaky hands.

Fargo was across the clearing before Charlie could get off a second wild shot, his first kick sending the man's pistol off into the night, and his second, right into the hollow spot at the base of his rib cage, slamming the man to his back and knocking the bleeding hunter unconscious.

Manuel Chico hadn't hollered for a while, and the mule had settled down. So Fargo checked there and wished he hadn't. It gave him a sick feeling in his stomach as a green taste climbed into his mouth and took over.

Chico's tight black twill pants were a tatter of bloody strips, almost indistinguishable from the shredded flesh of his legs in the flickering firelight. A big chunk had been gouged from his side, just above his hip, and smaller pieces of his chest had been nibbled away. Both arms had been flayed and scourged, although the man's lean, leathery face had generally escaped the attack.

The horses looked restive, but too tired to show their usual dismay about the odor of fresh blood. Maybe they figured it was okay if one of their own had caused it.

Miraculously, Chico's chest was still heaving, so Fargo dragged him and the unconscious Charlie over toward the fire. Laura was sitting on a log, petrified, her eyes clamped shut. Whenever she blinked them open, they had that glazed look of someone who's seen more than she ever wants to see again.

Lem Sloat hadn't managed to escape. The Turk had allowed him to get a few feet out of the clearing before jabbing the scimitar up the man's ass, not far enough to do any real damage. But enough to stop Sloat and allow the Turk to prod the owlhoot back toward the fire.

Ahmet didn't look at all flustered, so Fargo just stood there openmouthed while the foreign sergeant made a little speech. Lem was alert enough to hear it, tough old Charlie was coming around again, and it was a safe bet that the next thing Manuel Chico heard would be Old Nick welcoming him to an eternal roast in molten sulfur. But the man's shattered chest was still moving up and down, so there wasn't any way to be certain.

"Mr. Fargo over there tells me," Ahmet intoned like a teacher giving a lesson, "that he has some questions for which he desires some answers." He pointed the scimitar toward Slim's head, on the ground next to the fire. "That man can longer tell Mr. Fargo what he wishes to know. So one of you must."

The sword's tip materialized above Lem's outspread left hand. "I will start slow, just perhaps a finger at a time, until you decide to talk to Mr. Fargo. If the sword annoys you, I can arrange to use the fire on your hands."

The green taste returned to Fargo's mouth as he stepped over next to Ahmet and bent to whisper in his ear. "Ahmet, I can't say as I hold with torture. There's got to be a better way than your way."

"My way!" the Turk hissed back indignantly. "It was you barbaric Christians who taught us how to do this, back during the Crusades. Before that, we were a civilized people."

"But . . ." Fargo tried to interject.

The Turk's voice softened. "It is not my way either. But they do not know that. So let them think for a few minutes that I mean to slice and fry them. A threat is often more powerful than when you carry it through."

Fargo nodded, glad he and Ahmet were on the same side. The wiry, fearless Turk returned his attention to the sprawled men, no doubt noticing, as Fargo had, that Manuel Chico's battered torso had quit heaving.

"You"—Ahmet pointed with the blade—"why is it that you raid only certain caravans?" Chico, of course, didn't answer, so the blade lopped off a hand. The swift sound of metal slicing flesh was unmistakable, and Charlie couldn't see, from where he was trying to sit up, that Chico hadn't noticed.

Charlie got his left hand clamped over the hole in his right shoulder, slowing the bleeding, before he tried to answer. "Hey, wait," he grunted. "We're just hired men."

Ahmet spun and waved the sword near Charlie's groin. "If you do not wish to sing like a woman, then you tell us more."

With a tremendous agonized effort, Sloat coiled up, got his feet under him, and lunged toward Ahmet, who was standing too close in front of Fargo to allow the Trailsman to get off a shot in time. But it was kind of stupid to charge a man with a sword, anyway, because a moment later, the bloody tip was emerging from Sloat's back.

Impaled at arm's reach and down on his knees, Sloat flailed at the air as the Turk twisted the sword, its razor edge severing the man's spine. Ahmet withdrew the sword. His eyes wide with fright, Sloat watched it come out of his own belly, frozen in position until he toppled a moment later, face-first into the fire.

A scream more terrible than any yet that evening came out of the flames as Sloat waved his arms and tried to push himself out of the embers. He couldn't use his legs, Fargo realized, because his spinal cord had been cut and there was no longer any way for his burning brain to control the limbs.

"They insist on torturing themselves, no matter how nice I am," the Turk muttered as Fargo stepped around and put a bullet into Sloat's smoldering skull, then pulled at the man's legs until the body was out of the fire.

For whatever reasons, Charlie got more talkative after asking for a sip of water, which Laura brought him.

"Fargo," he finally said after collecting his thoughts and getting comfortable, his back against a log while his legs sprawled before him, "I think you found the only son of a bitch in New Mexico Territory that's meaner than Espinoza."

Ahmet grinned and bowed, finding himself nearly toppled by Laura's embrace. She said something warm and lustful about wanting to thank the man who'd rescued her from the trouble she'd gotten into on account of helping Fargo. It hadn't quite worked that way, but Fargo didn't see any reason to explain it all to her at the moment. And Ahmet had certainly earned his hour of pleasure.

Ignoring the giggles and heavy breathing from the woods just past the clearing, Fargo returned his attention to Charlie. The old hunter's lined face was ashen, his lips drawn inside a frame formed by a salt-and-pepper ring formed by his mustache and goatee, still quite distinct even though the man's cheeks hadn't been shaved for several days.

Still clutching his shoulder, Charlie sat up straighter. "Fargo, I'll tell you all I know. Which ain't a lot, Lord knows, but if it's all the same to you, mebbe it'll keep that Turk from fryin' me."

"It might," Fargo conceded, crouching down beside the wheezing man in patched buckskins.

" 'Twas the spring before this'n when I come through Cimarron an' stopped at Swink's," Charlie explained, "on my way from winterin' in Taos an' headin' for the Panhandle. An' I run into this Mex feller. Now, he wasn't much bigger'n a minute, the kind of guy that had to stand twice to cast a shadow, and he didn't look like he amounted to a hill of shit, shufflin' along in his serape."

The trouble with old hunters, trappers, scouts, and the like, Fargo decided, was that they'd spent too much time living among the Indians and had picked up some bad habits. There wasn't an Indian alive who could talk straight and to the point; they all rambled and took two or three hours to convey five minutes' worth of information, the rest of their talk consisting mostly of brag. Now that Charlie was wound up, he could no doubt talk most of the night, no matter how much blood he'd lost to the shoulder wound.

144

"That feller was Vicente Espinoza, an' he told me there was easier ways to make a livin' than killin' buffalo an' sellin' the hides. Well, there ain't many harder ways, Fargo, you know that? Ride for fuckin' ever, under a hot sun where there ain't no shade in a hunnert miles, fin'ly find some pissant little herd an' set up your stand, an' you gets no more'n five or six of 'em afore the herd spooks an' departs fer Canada. That's right, Canada, not just the Canadian River.

"So him an' me agreed that most anythin' this side of pickin' cotton was easier'n huntin' buffalo. An' we got to talkin' some, an' he said this feller over'n Santa Fe had offered him a most amazin' deal."

"Just how did that work?" Fargo asked.

"The way Espinoza explained it, this businessman in Santa Fe was willin' to pay—an' pay pretty—fer some bushwhackin' on certain wagon trains. He'd get word to us just which ones to hit, an' once they was hit, we could keep all we got, as well as gettin' paid."

"Any reason for it?" Fargo asked. "Was this Santa Fe man trying to get rid of business rivals, maybe?"

Charlie let loose a long, rattling sigh. "Mebbe somethin' like that. Way Espinoza talked, this Santa Fe man was mighty mad, said whoever was runnin' them trains was fixin' to steal whatever was most precious to him, or somethin' like that." Charlie wheezed and rattled some more.

Fargo stepped over to the canteen and brought it back. Charlie helped himself to a swallow, then continued.

"So that's how it come about. Espinoza rounded up some other fellers for the work, whenever somebody come through. He figured tongues would start waggin' if we was always hangin' out at Swink's, so we spent a lot o' rowdy nights up in the hills between jobs."

"You still caused some talk, judging by what I heard at Fort Union," Fargo said, gazing thoughtfully at the fire and trying to figure out how much truth there was in Charlie's tale, and if there was, just who, among all the rich, unscrupulous men in Santa Fe, might be the one who'd put this scheme to Espinoza.

"That's as might be," Charlie allowed, his voice growing faint and hoarse. "But nobody knew where to find us when we was out of town, layin' low, an' it just ain't natural fer a man not to visit a saloon ever' now an' again, if it's handy. You knows how that works, don't ya, Fargo?"

The man's voice drifted, along with his recollections of the better saloons of the West. As Charlie's voice continued to fade, Fargo bent low, hoping that the near whispers would return to the recent glory days of the Espinoza gang. Carelessly low, because Charlie's hand snaked out and grabbed the butt of the Trailsman's pistol.

He didn't manage to get it clear of the holster because Fargo's fist reflexively slammed the old coot's grasping, talonlike hand. As the pistol fell back, Charlie brought up a bony knee, straight into Fargo's jaw. Stunned by the gnarled hunter's swiftness, Fargo rolled back off the log, and by the time he was up and ready to fire, Charlie had scampered out of the clearing, into the woods.

Fargo shook his head in wonderment, looking carefully at where Charlie had been and where he'd gone. No, the smooth old bastard hadn't stopped to grab any guns, at least not that Fargo could notice. It was hard to be sure, given how sloppy this camp had become, what with bodies lying all around like the last act of *Hamlet*.

One reason Fargo was known for his tracking skills wasn't that he was good at reading sign. Not that he was bad at it, but generally the trail was the least important part of any tracking job. The important thing was to learn to think like your quarry, to run matters through your mind until you knew just what the man you were tracking would have to do. Once you had that figured out, you generally didn't need to follow the trail. You knew where your man was headed, and often you could be there waiting for him.

So Fargo stood there and took a couple of deep breaths to settle himself down and keep from feeling so damn mad at the way Charlie had suckered him. He knew he'd succeeded when he felt a smile of admiration start creeping across his face. That had been a hell of a trick.

Now, Charlie did have a hole in both sides of his shoulder, which hadn't done him much good. But the old bullshit artist was as tough as boot leather. So he'd be able to travel, some.

Fargo tried to figure out what he'd do in Charlie's place. Would he hang around camp, hoping somehow to triumph when he was outnumbered and outgunned? When there was nothing there for him anyway?

No, he'd light out for help, if there was any close by. Taking off on horseback wouldn't make much sense, no matter how bad Charlie felt, since the horses were exhausted from the hard riding of the past two days. A man would make better time afoot, at least until he could acquire a fresh mount by whatever means.

Where would Charlie go? Fargo thought back on all he'd been told, and it added up that Espinoza's mountain hideout was no more than ten miles away. Traveling at night and wounded, Charlie wouldn't get there before sunrise, and likely later if he got there at all. No matter how tough a man was, he needed some rest.

So did Fargo. Even though none of the other men in the clearing was in any condition to stir, it wasn't exactly restful. After feeding the fire, he started tidying up, grunting as he dragged Chico's battered body toward the edge, and grimacing when he saw the man's severed hand still near the fire, clutching the earth.

8

By the potent light of what promised to be another blistering day, Fargo had little trouble following Charlie's escape route. The tracks of a man who took off running and then ran out of steam led northward from the clearing that had become the last resting place for his three companions.

Or at least, Laura and Ahmet had said something about digging a common grave and then depositing the various remaining chunks of Slim, Manuel Chico, and Lem Sloat in it. Later on during their sunrise breakfast, Fargo said he'd chase Charlie down. Ahmet promised they'd be coming along after they'd broken camp.

Even a wounded man on foot could make better time than they would with three tired horses, a chain-hating mule, and Alkazar the camel. Persuading the horseflesh and the camel to stay within sight of one another promised to be a chore. This was up-and-down rough country, heavily forested in spots and broken up by east-trending steep-walled ravines that were too big to be gulches and too small to be real canyons. It just wasn't built for good riding.

Fargo paused at the crest of yet another ravine to marvel at the old buffalo hunter's stamina. He also explained to the Ovaro that even though the big pinto was tired from all the recent hard riding, there wasn't any cause to complain about this morning's excursion. Thanks to the trees and the general rough nature of Charlie's route, Fargo might have spent all of twenty minutes out of the past three hours in the saddle. His horse ought to understand that this was just a mutual walk, not a workout.

Next to Fargo, a towering ponderosa bore several finger-sized dark stains on its rough bark, about chest high. The Trailsman recognized them as blood. Charlie had doubtless staggered up here—his footprints had been kind of wobbly for the past quarter-mile—and leaned against the tree to catch his breath while that shoulder wound dripped some against the tree.

Now it was getting easier to outthink the old rascal. Suppose Charlie had just been trying to get the hell away from a deadly neighborhood. In that case, he'd have worked his way to the first likely gulch, then worked his way down it toward the plains that stretched eastward. He wouldn't have to go far before finding a ranch head-quarters. There he could either bullshit his way into some help, or just steal a horse. Either way, he could hie himself to the nearby settlement of Cimarron, where hard cases could rest up in friendly surroundings.

Suppose Charlie was still being sneaky and devious. If so, he'd have led Fargo down a gulch toward some suit-able ambush spot. The man couldn't be toting anything much bigger than a derringer. So he'd have to set himself in a brush-filled hollow where he'd be reasonably sure of getting a close shot at Fargo. That hadn't happened, either.

So the sign all indicated that the battered buffalo hunter was heading for the nearest help he could count on. That would be the mountain hideout he'd mentioned to Fargo last night when he'd been talking like a dying man and waiting for a chance to grab Fargo's Colt and light out. Fargo reckoned that Charlie sometimes slipped up and said something truthful. Nobody was perfect.

Even the prospect of finding that hideout didn't make the pursuit any less tedious, though. It was just some sweaty walking up and down some rough country.

Breakfast had totally worn off and Fargo's belly was starting to think that his throat had been slit when he told it to quit growling. "You just behave till we top the next rise," he muttered, "and I'll reward you with some jerky and parched corn." As soon as he topped this narrow ridge, he started reaching in the saddlebags. The Ovaro started acting as skittish as a bear on roller skates.

Fargo saw Charlie's tired tracks lead down the powdery slope toward the brush-lined creek at the bottom. No matter how carefully he scanned the opposite side, he couldn't be sure that there were tracks up it. The sun was now high and right behind him. There just weren't any shadows to define such impressions as the sand might be holding. Fargo sniffed, but there wasn't anything to smell besides his sweat and the horse's in the breezeless air.

The Ovaro had his ears cocked, so Fargo tried that, cupping his hands behind his own ears. At first all he heard was a tiny creek straining to get from pool to pool through the rocks. Then the distant buzz of flies, at first indistinct, became clear, almost annoying.

Everything told him that this was Charlie's last valley. That suspicion that was confirmed when Fargo, Colt in hand and stepping warily, finally arrived amid the sharp-pointed willow branches. The hunter's shoulder wound had come open again, and he'd stopped to rest next to the creek. The flies buzzed delightedly in the congealed blood, and the man's unprotected face was staring up at the brutal sun. He'd never be getting up again.

Recalling how Charlie had deceived him last night, Fargo felt a powerful temptation to put a bullet through the man's skull, just to be sure. As it was, though, the buzzards would be along any minute for today's lunch.

After gaining the next ridge and placating his own hunger, Fargo was glad he hadn't made any noise by firing a needless shot.

From that rise, he saw a well-used trail along the bottom, next to a creek more substantial than anything he'd seen all morning. Staying on the ridge for a mile or so on west into the looming mountains, Fargo was rewarded with the sight of Vicente Espinoza's mountain hideout.

It wasn't much. In a pocket where the valley widened into a lush meadow surrounded by forest, there stood a solid log cabin. It was perhaps twenty by twenty, roofed with shake shingles split out of jack pine and sorely in need of a coat of linseed oil.

Through the waving knee-high grass, one path led from the cabin door over to a pole corral that held four horses. Another beaten track connected the cabin to a slab-walled privy that was almost in the trees. It was lunchtime, which explained the blue-gray wood smoke wafting out through a rusty stovepipe poked through the roof.

Fargo eyed his Sharps in the saddle boot. With its range, he'd have no trouble picking off somebody from up here. After the first shot, though, the others could get forted up good in the cabin. They'd just end up in a long standoff.

Leaving the Ovaro up on the ridge to stare enviously at the rich bottom grass, Fargo worked his way noiselessly through the woods. He settled down in the trees behind the unpainted two-holer. His tensed legs hadn't even started to complain when a lanky man sporting a full brown beard strolled his way. In a hand that was missing a little finger, he carried a newspaper.

He didn't get a chance to read or wipe with it. As soon as the outhouse blocked the man's view, Fargo sprang out from behind, wheeled around the privy, and just followed the man inside. He jammed his Colt against the man's spine as he pulled the door shut behind them.

Fargo wanted to explain the considerable advantages of an extended conversation, but the lanky fellow tried to twist and go for his own gun. Fargo didn't want to shoot and draw the attention of the others finishing lunch in the cabin, but he didn't see as he had much choice if he planned to even the odds against him here.

At such close range, the man's lean body did muffle most of the muzzle blast. He was thin enough to be shoved headfirst down one of the openings in the privy bench. Fargo had to ram hard, though, to get the last of the man's boots pushed below the bench. Figuring he might as well take advantage of what was available, Fargo settled onto the adjacent rim and studied on the newspaper while reliving himself.

Soon Fargo stood and adjusted his trousers, remembering that he had work to do. There were probably three more hard cases sitting comfortably in a cabin not twenty yards away.

Make that two left in the cabin. Fargo heard something stirring in the yard and peeked out through a crack. A brown-skinned man of average height and build, clean-shaven as a baby and dressed vaquero-style in black, had come outside. He looked edgy as he kept a nervous hand on his holstered pistol. "Hey, Buck!" he called out. "Did you fall in?"

Fargo looked at the warped plank walls and decided they were perfectly suitable for a shithouse, but not worth a plugged nickel in hell for protection. Bullets would sail right through these thin boards. Going the other way, he'd never be sure of one clean killing shot if he were trying to fire his Colt out through a knothole.

Making his voice sound strained and hurt, Fargo hollered back. "Jesus, I think something bit me. Stings like hell and I can't move worth mention."

"Tarantula," the outside man countered. "A big hairy spider bit me once, too. Sit tight. I'll get Clem. We'll bring you inside."

Clem and Clean-shaven arrived a minute or two later, Clem in the lead. He of course had to lean some on the outhouse door, since there was a latch. Both stumbled right on in when Fargo released the latch. Neither was in any position to argue with the Trailsman's pistol butt. Both went down and out.

Working quickly with his knife, Fargo fabricated some gags and ties out of Clem's denim trousers. He left the two lying in the outhouse, one on the floor and one on the bench. Just how long they'd stay out was questionable. The place had a stench that might have roused Charlie.

Fargo circled the cabin and tried to spy through a window. The cabin had one. It was even made out of glass. But it was typical New Mexico primitive, made out of old bottles jammed together. All it was good for was letting in light. In the dim interior, someone was sitting at a table but any further detail would require closer inspection.

When Fargo went around and walked in the door, Colt

drawn, the short heavy-set Mexican inside had stepped over to the stove. He was pouring himself some more coffee. Cocking his head ever so slightly, he saw the gun and whirled like a tornado, flinging boiling coffee at Fargo as he ducked and rolled.

Fargo's thick and unruly beard kept most of his face from getting scalded by the stream. His eyelids clamped shut to protect his continued vision, so he couldn't catch the coffee-thrower's exact location. Lunging sightlessly, Fargo threw himself on inside the cabin.

Twisting and diving as he opened his eyes, he got off three hurried shots. Two thudded harmlessly into the log walls, and the third hit the cast-iron stove and ricocheted, splatting into his opponent's back.

The prone man had been stretched, his arms before him and his pistol coming up for an easy shot at Fargo. As the Trailsman got his bearings, he saw the pistol drop. The man tried to get up on all fours, then sighed. He sagged and collapsed in the pool of blood that dripped from a fist-sized hole in his chest. That was where Fargo's bouncing bullet had come out.

Wishing that his scalded nose and brow would quit stinging and settle down to just aching, Fargo stepped across the packed dirt floor, holding his breath. The cabin smelled damn near as rank as the outhouse, and it might have been even filthier.

The shot had been lucky, sure enough. Fargo traced the ding on the side of the cast-iron stove to the butterfly-shaped hole in the man's heaving back. But if the Trailsman's luck was really running good today, the wounded man would be Vicente Espinoza, and he'd have some deathbed confessions to make.

Trouble was, the man wasn't Vicente and he wasn't talking to anybody while he gasped and heaved his dying breaths. He stared at the floor and finally quit rattling after a couple minutes.

After going down to the creek and washing his burned face in cold water until it felt numb, Fargo dragged the man's carcass out of the cabin and studied on his next step.

In a way, he'd finished his job. Espinoza's men had

definitely been the raiders of Ashford's wagon trains. Now Espinoza's gang was pretty well out of commission, no matter where Vicente might be lurking at the moment. But somebody had paid Espinoza to give up petty theft and harassment in order to go after Ashbrook's wagons exclusively, to commit the atrocious Barclay Massacre.

Fargo suspected he could put the two men in the outhouse on spits and roast them over a slow fire, and they still wouldn't be able to tell him any more than he already knew: that Vicente had cut some kind of deal with a business sort from Santa Fe. Which meant there were only two or three hundred possibilities in that city of intrigue where nothing was as it appeared to be.

Fargo knew he could track down Espinoza if it came to that. But it sure as hell wouldn't be easy. Spanish-speaking folks hereabouts tended to look upon him as their very own Robin Hood, stealing from the rich Anglos who'd stolen their land and destroyed their traditional livelihoods. They'd shelter and succor him while making life difficult for Fargo.

But even if Espinoza showed up at the door right now and Fargo put him away, it wouldn't really solve Ashbrook's problem. Whoever was putting Espinoza's gang up to these outrages could just find another group of drifters, hard cases, outlaws, bail jumpers, army deserters, riffraff, and the like. It wouldn't be hard at all in New Mexico Territory to assemble a new cutthroat gang for theft and murder. A man could do that in less than an afternoon of buying beer at Swink's Saloon in Cimarron or any cantina in Taos.

It was small consolation to find out how right he'd been thinking when he hauled the trussed-up men out of the outhouse and got them to talking.

Other than Vicente, they insisted, the whole gang was now dead or captured. Vicente did all the thinking and dealing, and they just took orders. The last they'd seen of him was two nights ago when he'd headed north. He hadn't said where he was going, only that he'd return within the week.

North meant the outlaw would soon strike the old trail

over Palo Flechado Pass. He could swing east a dozen miles to Cimarron, or west over the mountains to Taos. Which meant the wily rogue could be pretty well anywhere.

At least Clem Whitlock and José Archileta had consented to talk halfway friendly with Fargo. He wasn't sure what to do with them. He couldn't persuade himself that he should kill them in cold blood, even if that's what they'd helped do to Hank Barclay and the others on that wagon train less than a fortnight ago. He wouldn't feel right about leaving them loose anywhere to get in more trouble, either. And he'd feel even less right about taking two such shady characters with him, wherever he went next once he figured out what he was going to go.

Hearing a commotion up the hill, Fargo looked that way and felt his face crack his first smile of the day. As promised, Ahmet and Laura had arrived. Or were trying to. The swarthy man in robes had to divide his attention. He'd cuss the camel in the guttural Turkish for a while, then he'd swear at the mule in fluent English before devoting more harsh words to the camel.

Meanwhile Laura, about a hundred yards ahead, was leading the three outlaw horses. When she spied Fargo, she gave an excited wave and traipsed down through the trees, her ample breasts heaving through the linen robe she still wore.

By overhauling the smallest outlaw's boots, she and Ahmet had managed some sandals, Fargo noticed before turning his eyes upward toward more pleasing parts of her anatomy.

"I'm so glad to see you, Skye," she uttered between deep, heaving breaths, collapsing against him with an exuberant embrace. The way she was rubbing against his crotch, she had to know how glad he was to see her.

"Thought you and Ahmet were getting along fine," he said, rubbing her shoulders as he returned her tight bear hug.

"Let's just say that we're still friends," she said, "but, er, well, we have different tastes. He's a little too exotic for a small-town gal like me."

Fargo didn't try to speculate as to what Ahmet might have expected from this good-natured professional woman.

155

She was kissing him like she planned to pull his tongue out by its roots once she'd prospected every bit of his mouth.

When he came up for air, he saw that Ahmet was tying the camel and mule over at the edge of the clearing. Laura's three horses had already made their own way down to the lush grass. Recalling that the Ovaro was still up there, Fargo whistled and untangled himself from Laura.

He walked over toward the busy Turk, hoping that they were still pals and still on the same side. Misunderstandings with and about women had a way of ruining friendships between men.

But Ahmet, his dark eyes flashing as he straightened, seemed philosophical. "Ah, Fargo," he said, extending his hand, "I see you didn't need our help here, after all."

They jawed some, and Fargo mentioned he'd read in the paper about a skirmish with the Mexican army down in Texas.

The Turk smiled, his white teeth glistening in his sweat-soaked black beard. "Good. Finally I might get to fight instead of herd camels for you strange Yankees. I'll have to return to duty, I guess." The Turk seemed anxious to head back. "This has been fun, Fargo. You lead a most interesting life and I am most thankful to you for sharing some of it with me." He surveyed the clearing, then pointed at the body near the cabin. "Is that dead man your Espinoza?"

Fargo shook his head. "He lit out a couple days ago. Them two tied up over there told me all they have to say, and there's another standing on his head in the shithouse hole. That pretty well accounts for the gang."

The Turk laughed some while Fargo explained how his nose and forehead had gotten scalded to a glowing crimson that afternoon. Scanning the sky and noticing there was still considerable daylight left, Ahmet asked how far it might be down to Cimarron, and if there was any kind of decent trail where a man could ride a camel, rather than pull it.

Satisfied that it was only a mile or two to the Palo Flechado Pass, which would give him easy riding to Cim-

arron and points south and east, the Turk untied Alkaz
and bade the camel to kneel. "May Allah be with you
Fargo."

"Good luck yourself," Fargo said, waving as Ahmet
departed down the well-used trail that led out of the
valley. Sending the two gang members and Laura along
with him as far as Cimarron might save some time, Fargo
thought, but the Turk played kind of rough all the way
around.

So it was just as well that he and Laura had the
clearing to themselves that night, with the two varmints
penned inside the cabin after Fargo had checked their
manacles, shoved them inside, and nailed the door shut.
Outside beat hell out of inside when inside was filthy and
full of lice, bedbugs, roaches, and other disgusting critters. Clem and José were no doubt used to it, anyway.

After a hearty and early supper, Laura spread the bedroll out on the grass. It was still broad daylight when she
cuddled up next to him and slithered out of her robe
while working her hands under his clothes.

"Oh, Skye," she kept murmuring, "I'm so glad to be
back with you."

Fargo felt more than a twinge of curiosity as to the
exact cause of her disagreement with Ahmet's style of
lovemaking, but he wasn't about to ask. Part of it was
manners. But most of it was that when he was in bed
with a woman, the last thing he wanted to hear was how
he compared with any other men she'd known. Even
though women generally said nice things about him, it
just didn't sit right.

But Laura was sitting right. She wriggled his trousers
down to half-mast and rolled a smooth thigh over the
part of him that was at full mast, impaling herself with a
plunge that took Fargo deep into a satisfying moistness.

He started bucking some, just to give her a better ride.
Meanwhile he enjoyed the close-up view of her bobbing
full breasts, erect nipples floating ahead of rosy areolae
that spread back into creamy white roundness, fading so
slowly that a man couldn't really say where one ended
and the other started.

She leaned down, grabbing his shoulders. Moments

157

.ter, he reached up and pulled her to him. Their rhythm continued undisturbed even as they rolled over to put him on top. She got real excited, apparently trying to hook her feet against Fargo's ears while he pounded in, deeper with every stroke.

Laura was the first to climax, just about the time the setting sun finally put them in the cooling shadows. Every muscle inside and out got tight and even tighter. Her arms encircled him with a grip that would have shamed a grizzly bear. Her thighs, arched up to flank his chest, added to the pleasant pressure as she kicked her legs up to lock her ankles over Fargo's waving back, catching his torso in a scissors grip. Fargo could feel the internal tightening pressure of her frenzy as each stroke took longer than the last.

Rolling her back some more, Fargo knew he was as far in as a man ever figured to get, but he pushed onward, just to be sure. She quivered like an aspen leaf in a windstorm, then cut loose with a yell no doubt heard on the other side of the mountains.

When Fargo recalled that there was still a world out there, just past his back, he glanced around nervously and saw that the horses hadn't been bothered worth mention by her outburst. Returning his attention to the shuddering woman whose sweat-stained eager face was swirling in a cloud of ruddy curls, he felt a surge of relief, with the force of a dam breaking, pour over him as he fired round after round deep inside. She didn't mind a bit as she kept up the satisfied moaning that sounded like the purr of a big cat.

They did stop for breath after that, but the darker it got outside, the wilder Laura got. Along about midnight, Fargo couldn't imagine a thing that Ahmet might have tried with Laura that they hadn't done. But then again, maybe the man had just wanted some sleep, which seemed to be way down on her list of desires.

Fargo felt kind of relieved midway through the next morning as he and Laura parted friendly on a dusty street in Cimarron. He knew he'd be missing her warmth within a night or two, but there just wasn't any practical way to take her along what promised to be one gritty ar hard ride.

Espinoza hadn't been seen around town for better than a week, according to gossip from several sources ranging from the livery stable to the barbershop to several hangers-on at Swink's. Which meant heading back into the mountains and going hell-bent to Taos, as soon as he finished his morning chores.

Fargo deposited two retired road agents with the local sheriff, whose stone-walled jail looked more substantial than his honesty or dedication to justice. The fellow at the livery stable was more than willing to buy the mule and take in the three horses. He was so friendly that Fargo took the trouble to mention the mule's dislike of chains rattling within earshot.

After those errands, Laura said that joining Fargo had worked out as pleasure for her, rather than a professional duty, so he had to argue some to get her to accept a few double-eagles. She'd need a stake and some travel money to set up here or wherever, Fargo reasoned. It was his fault that she wasn't still in business down by Fort Union, fifty miles away. When this had all started, all she was supposed to do was entertain a shavetail for thirty minutes.

Finally taking the coins and agreeing that they both had separate careers to pursue, she said she hoped they'd meet again. Fargo hoped so too and headed west on the Ovaro.

He didn't dare push the big pinto, not with all the recent hard riding, so the sixty-mile trip across the mountains took longer than he would have liked. But if a man wanted his horse to take care of him, then he had to take care of his horse. So they spent two nights on the trail before getting into Taos one afternoon, and he promised his mount an extended rest there.

The Trailsman had never minded hanging around Taos, anyway. And the oats provided at the livery stable were no doubt healthier than the whiskey provided at the adobe-walled cantinas that sat around the dusty plaza.

This sleepy village was a good place to join the Ovaro in loafing and resting up. But it wasn't the place where a stranger like Fargo could just ride in and start firing questions about Vicente Espinoza. Taos wasn't a trade center like Santa Fe, or a trail town like Las Vegas or Cimarron, places where Anglo strangers came and went all the time.

The local residents felt suspicious about any tall, blue-eyed man who might ride in and want information about a man whom they considered one of their own. The Indians in nearby Taos Pueblo were even more close-mouthed. There wasn't any overt hostility, but there was a wall, invisible but impossible to breach, that sprang up between Fargo and nearly everyone he met once the conversation got much past *"Buenos días."*

Even the livery stable and the saloons, places where a man who remained alert while looking bored could generally hear something of interest, offered little more than the usual chatter, and precious little of that. He did gather that Espinoza came through Taos with some regularity.

One friendly farrier who trimmed the Ovaro's hooves laughingly admitted that he didn't know Vicente Espinoza from Adam's off ox. But he recalled that a couple months ago, he'd seen a serape-clad nondescript fellow, one he hadn't seen around town, jawing considerable with a dapper-dressed gringo who had close-cropped sandy hair and a waxed mustache, also somebody not often seen in Taos.

It could have been Espinoza. And it could have been ten thousand other men.

Frustrated after days of loafing, Fargo was about ready to move on anyway late one afternoon when a short wagon train pulled into the plaza.

It had come up from Santa Fe with trade goods for Taos. Even through the cloud of dust, he had no trouble recognizing one of the mule skinners as Ugly Jack. Fargo's offer of a drink inside a shady cantina was gladly accepted.

By hustling here and there, Fargo learned, Ashbrook had put together some recently arrived Santa Fe goods and sent a four-wagon caravan up the Rio Grande valley for a three-day trip to Taos. Which explained why Ugly Jack was here and why there was a crowd gathering in the plaza, already lining up to buy everything from ha▮ combs to bullet molds.

Ugly Jack hadn't seen any notorious Mex bandits along the way. Hadn't seen much of anybody, for all that. The big talk around his part of Santa Fe was Phoebe Ashbrook.

"She was some looker, warn't she?" Jack confided.

Fargo nodded, wondering why he was referring to Phoebe in the past tense.

"You know, she was always moanin' an' bitchin' 'bout how cut off an' uncouth Santa Fe is," Jack continued, draining his shot glass of tequila and waving it at the waitress, "but I reckon she's found herself a man that suits her high-toned tastes."

"Who would that be?" Fargo asked, gritting his teeth every time Jack opened his nearly toothless mouth. That wouldn't have been so bad, but the remaining half-dozen cutters and grinders were yellow fading to brown.

"Ever run across that Lord Cavendish gent when you was in town?"

Biting his tongue to keep from mentioning Perk Doyle, Fargo grunted agreement and finished his own shot of fiery tequila.

"They're gettin' hitched. Ol' man's throwin' a big weddin' with all the trimmin's, likely a considerable dowry too, being as she's tyin' up with a real limey lord or baron or what have you. She's all aflutter. Got herself a cultured man that's gone to college at Oxford."

Fargo stared at the nicked wooden tabletop before daring to raise his eyes to meet Ugly Jack's scarred face. He didn't know whether to laugh or get sick. Pretentious Phoebe had sure enough found her match, a marriage that figured to last until Doyle gambled his way through her dowry. Although that might take years, or maybe forever, given the man's skill with a deck of cards.

"The ol' man's pleased as punch about it all," Jack continued, "but that Fletcher shithead that had his heart set on her is fit to be tied. Remember how you told me to keep him busy that afternoon? That sissy acted too good to shovel shit out of stalls. Had to wave a pitchfork at him to persuade that fancy-pants that his back'd bend just as good as anybody else's."

Another round arrived, and Ugly Jack went on about what a snooty asshole Billy Fletcher was, but Fargo suddenly lost interest as the wheels started to turn and click in his head. Rising, he tossed some coins on the table. "Jack, it was good to see you. But I've got to run. Likely I'll see you in Santa Fe when you get back."

The rested Ovaro almost seemed to welcome the challenge, and the broad but winding route along the west flank of the Sangres ran generally downhill anyway. The gibbous moon provided sufficient light, and the night air was crisp and bracing without ever turning downright chilly.

Through ancient sleeping villages like Chamisal and Chimayo, past long-abandoned pueblos whose crumbling mud-brick walls shimmered in the silvery moonlight, Fargo and the big pinto covered the sixty miles to Santa Fe without incident. They didn't even have to push hard to arrive at the territorial capital not long after the sun, and neither was too much the worse for wear. Fargo rubbed down his mount and found a stall for him in Ashbrook's stable, then caught a two-hour nap when he realized he'd made better time than expected.

Finding Vicente Espinoza anywhere in New Mexico Territory would be like finding one tree in a vast forest, the way the man could melt into the countryside. Fargo studied on that while strolling up the street, the morning dew still so fresh that it wasn't yet dusty. But the man's gang was shattered. And Ashbrook's wagons would roll back and forth with no more than the usual disturbances if Fargo could find the man who'd put Espinoza up to the raids.

He found the man he wanted, sitting at Phoebe's old table toward the rear wall of the Ashbrook emporium.

As soon as Fargo came through the front door from the plaza, Fletcher got the look of a cat that had just swallowed the canary. But he managed to stand up, looking friendly enough to shake hands by the time Fargo was inside with the door slammed behind him.

"Mr. Fargo," Fletcher announced. "I'm glad you're back so soon."

Mildly surprised at the greeting, Fargo just nodded and kept his hand atop his Colt.

"I want to hire you," Fletcher said, his voice growing firmer.

"Can't imagine there's anything that a tumbleweed drifter could do for an important man of your standing," Fargo spat.

"You've got to bring Phoebe to me. She won't see me, won't talk to me, and I'm losing her." The man's voice started shaking some. "Losing her to a tinhorn that has everybody fooled into thinking he's British gentry."

"Lord Cavendish is a handsome, wealthy man," Fargo consoled, stepping closer to the trembling Fletcher.

"He's not a lord at all," Fletcher insisted. "She was supposed to marry me. I offered. God knows I begged the woman. She said she'd never be happy here, though." Fletcher sagged back into the wooden chair, resting his chin on his cupped hands and looked mournful. "I told her I'd take her back East, where she could have her concerts and poetry readings and all that, and she said she couldn't leave. Not while her father still wanted her in Santa Fe."

This was starting to sound confusing and Fargo even felt some sympathy for the man. But then he remembered that Hank Barclay had been his friend.

"So you decided to put Cyrus out of business in Santa Fe, the Santa Fe she hated so much," Fargo said as he shifted over to the side of the room away from the counter, where he had a wall to put against his back. "Then she'd be grateful to you because she'd get to go to the opera every Saturday night. So grateful that she'd marry you."

Fletcher's slack-jawed nod confirmed that Fargo had it right. It was an idiot scheme hatched by an arrogant but lovestruck man who was sure he could rearrange the world so that it ran according to his own wishes.

Billy wanted Phoebe. Phoebe wanted to leave Santa Fe, but wouldn't as long as her father had his business here. So put the old man out of business. Phoebe could leave. And she'd be so grateful to Billy that she'd marry him. Fargo tried to remember the last time he'd happened across something half as stupid, but recalled that it had been some years since he'd paid any mind to politics.

The man's tormented face fell to the table as he buried his head in his arms, his body racked by shudders and sobs. Fargo just stood there, watching Billy Fletcher torture himself. "How was I to know?" he kept asking the table, choking as his fingers alternately clenched and relaxed, never getting a grip on the smooth surface no matter how hard he pressed his fingertips against the polished wood.

"How were you to know what?" Fargo asked.

"Know that there'd be all that killing. I never, never thought that it would . . ." He was incoherent again and didn't have much choice but to listen to Fargo.

"Man never does know, except that when you start out doing something crooked, it'll get worse a long time before it gets better. You got your bright idea last summer, after the first raid, which was just one of those things as happens."

Fargo scanned the surroundings and collected his thoughts before proceeding. "Somehow you tipped that gang off that your employer's herd of mules wasn't all that well-guarded and was easy pickings. Cyrus stayed right here and Phoebe kept on being disgusted by Santa Fe. So you were in on that winter warehouse raid, which didn't make the Ashbrooks leave, either. With some of those proceeds, you hired Vicente Espinoza to make sure Ashford's summer caravan never arrived. And now you're all surprised and shook up when it strikes you that an outlaw don't play by the rules."

Fargo had been guessing some, but he knew he was right when Fletcher sat straight up. "Oh, Jesus," the man said to no one in particular. "He'll want more." Billy turned toward the Trailsman, his bloodshot teary eyes getting more glazed by the second as his mind started to unhinge. "Help me, Fargo."

There wasn't much chance to ask for details. Fargo had been watching Fletcher, or he'd have had a little more warning about what came easing through the front door: a little fellow in baggy cotton pants and a serape, who might have passed for harmless if it hadn't been for the wild gleam in his brown eyes and the long-barreled pistol that appeared in his right hand.

Standing against the wall, Fargo hadn't been visib. from the street. Vicente Espinoza, his eyes adjusting from the bright sunlight, at first saw only Billy Fletcher.

"Don't stall me off any longer, you gringo welsher," he hissed. "Where's the rest of my money?"

Fletcher started to turn in his chair, his arm loosely swinging across the tabletop. About that time, Espinoza caught sight of Fargo over by the wall, Colt in hand. The bandit must have thought Fletcher was going to come around with a gun.

His first bullet shattered Fletcher's shoulder blade, spinning the man around before he topped off his chair and thudded onto the floor. Fargo got off his own shot, right where Espinoza's chest had been a moment earlier, but it just creased the wiry man's side because he was dodging like a skeeter near a lantern.

Fargo hadn't stayed still either, so the Espinoza's second shot just settled into the adobe wall, raising a cloud of gritty dust, about a yard above Fargo's prone form. The Trailsman rolled away from the dust and smoke and caught sight of Espinoza springing up from a crouch, heading for the door.

If he got out, he'd disappear. Fargo's angle was terrible for a running shot, but there wasn't time to get up. His first bullet shattered a front window. The second, a moment later, was lower than he'd wanted.

But it was high enough to tear a gaping hole at the base of Espinoza's spine, right where a tail would have sprouted if men grew tails. The outlaw's legs immediately quit working and folded up under him. His free hand desperately clawed at the door frame for support as he sank. The other hand tried to bring the pistol around on Fargo, who snapped off another shot, the bullet punching a hole just above Vicente's navel.

Espinoza was tougher to kill than a snake, for he was still conscious, although breathing rough, when Fargo stepped over to him after noting that Billy Fletcher was too stunned and shocked to be a problem.

"Hey, Fargo," Espinoza whispered hoarsely. "Was a good fight, *sí?*"

Fargo nodded. *"Sí,"* he finally said. There were tough

men, brave men, men who loved the battle. They weren't good men or fair men, but you had to respect them. Sometimes they were on your side, like Ahmet, and sometimes they weren't, like Vicente. "It was a good fight," he told the dying outlaw.

Espinoza's last words tumbled out. "I did it for my people."

Fargo shook his head sadly as he rose. Vicente could have done a lot more for his people if he'd rounded them up at gunpoint and made then learn how to read, write, and otherwise get along in the new society that had been forced upon them, instead of terrorizing gringos. But the tough little cuss didn't know any other way except the hard way.

The commotion had attracted a crowd out in the plaza, although they were all standing a respectful distance from the storefront. Fargo glanced out and moved on back, where the bleeding Billy Fletcher was coming round with a nasty hole that had ruined his vest and linen shirt.

He was groaning how he'd done this all for Phoebe. She probably wouldn't appreciate the right arm he was going to lose on her account any more than she'd appreciate anything else Billy had ever tried to do for her.

Fargo made his way out the front door, almost bumping into some folks who were edging forward now that things had quieted down inside. He grabbed the first man he saw by the shoulders and told him to go fetch a doctor for a bleeding man inside, and stepped on through the crowd. Something about his surly expression warned curious bystanders not to ask him any questions. In fact, they were scurrying out of his path.

Fargo spotted Cyrus Ashbrook's portly frame hustling across the plaza, coming toward him. Keeping things simple, Fargo gave the merchant a quick explanation. Vicente Espinoza's gang had been responsible for the raids, and they were all dead, save for two that might still be in jail in Cimarron. Vicente himself was dead in a shoot-out, wherein Billy Fletcher had been seriously injured. The doctor was coming.

The astonished Ashbrook just kept shaking his jowls and pumping Fargo's hand. "Marvelous," he enthused.

166

"I knew you were the man for the job. You can tell m~
all about it at dinner tonight."

That sounded fair to Fargo, who planned to find a
room, a bath, and a drink, not necessarily in that order.
But as he stepped away, he saw Deputy Marshal Virgil
Clanborne hauling ass up the street his way, wheezing
some but still able to shout something about Skye Fargo
being under arrest for assaulting an officer, creating a
disturbance, murder, and other crimes too numerous to
mention.

Fargo legged it toward a side street, knowing that
Clanborne would just have to check out the carnage in
Ashbrook's store. Strolling along that street was a pleasant sight, his pal Laura, who'd arrived with a wagon train
only yesterday.

A practical woman, she'd already found a room, and
she said Fargo was just the man to help her break it in
for business. They ambled along toward the less-respectable
part of town, but didn't get far.

Out of a shady alley sprang a seething Carmelita.
"Fargo! My Fargo!" she screeched. "No white bitch takes
you from me this time!"

All teeth and fingernails, she launched herself toward
Laura. Fargo kind of liked the way Carmelita's heaving
bosom felt when he reached around to pull her off, and
the way her bobbing butt rubbed against his crotch wasn't
unpleasant either. But he wasn't making progress worth
mention until Laura managed an uppercut to Carmelita's
jaw and she sagged back and reeled some.

While Carmelita was still trying to get her bearings,
Fargo grabbed Laura's arm and took off running the two
blocks over to Ashbrook's stable. Even if the Ovaro was
tired from last night's long ride, he'd get them up to a
nearby glen in the mountains that Fargo remembered
fondly.

At the edge of town, Fargo tipped his hat to a tony
couple aboard a passing phaeton and offered his congrat-
ulations to Lord Cavendish and his bride-to-be, Phoebe
Ashbrook.

They seemed kind of snooty, Fargo thought, acting
like they didn't know him. But there was some justice,

e mused, even if he still wasn't good enough for society
in Santa Fe. Billy Fletcher was likely going through pure
hell right about now, getting his right arm sawed off
while he was wide awake with men holding him down,
and then a lifetime of getting by on just one arm. Most of
the others were dead. In a way, Phoebe Ashbrook had
started all this, and now she'd found her perfect, cultivated, educated husband—a riverboat gambler.

And then again, maybe Phoebe and her fiancé hadn't
recognized him on account of the saucy way Laura was
perched in front of him and bouncing her uncorseted
rump against his lap. It was all he could do to persuade
her to wait until they'd passed the last adobe *casa* until
she unbuttoned his fly and hoisted the skirt, so that it
fluttered down as she settled down. Laura made riding
double a pure pleasure.

LOOKING FORWARD!

**The following is the opening
section from the next novel in the exciting
Trailsman series from Signet:**

THE TRAILSMAN # 74
WHITE HELL

*Winter, 1860–61. The Salmon River Mountains,
Idaho, where prospectors gambled life against cunning
savagery and the raw, whirling fury of icy storm-death . . .*

The weather was still clear when Skye Fargo rode out of the settlement of Kooskia.

He knew, however, these quiet days of pale-gold sunshine couldn't last. He was in foothill country near the northern end of the brutally rugged Salmon River Mountains, and he could see the fine, thick growth of bunchgrass through the snow. It had taken on its winter color, gray, with a faint tinge of blue. To an Easterner this land of rounded slopes and broad canyons would have seemed a stony wasteland, incapable of supporting much life. But this was part of the Clearwater Basin winter range, and with the coming of snow, which made the cattle independent of rivers and water holes, numerous herds of independent ranchers started to arrive.

Fargo headed westward on the Lolo Indian Trail, which Lewis and Clark had followed back in 1805. He sighted a line cabin late that afternoon, and another the following day; and along toward early sundown of that second day, e noticed that the wind was changing. It had been blowing fitfully in from the south, but now it shifted, became steady, and when Fargo looked toward the "weather pot" in the northwest where this new wind originated, he saw that a silvery haze hung there.

The haze gathered bulk by the moment, rising higher and higher, till it caught up the sun and quenched it. Now it came scudding forward, high overhead, blotting out the sky, swooping low to obliterate distant stands of timber. It began to moan, and soon it was laden with small, compact pellets of snow.

Fargo dug heels into the flanks of his Ovaro and glanced over his shoulder at his trailing packhorse, a Roman-nosed dun gelding. The wind was developing into gale proportions. He drew on his slicker, turned up the collar, and tucked the sleeves into the flaring cuffs of gauntlet gloves.

The flakes of snow were larger now, and they drove past Fargo in great swarms, like stampeding white butterflies. Soon he was surrounded by gray darkness, and the cold was pressing in with chilling ferocity.

Suddenly the packhorse floundered, jerking on the lead rope, and Fargo turned leaning to look behind him. The combination of the packhorse yanking and Fargo leaning was enough to force the Ovaro to lurch off-balance, and before he could recover, his mount had slipped out from under him.

Fargo missed his grab for the horn, went spinning across the Ovaro's neck, then rolled with fierce energy when he struck the loose snow because he feared the horse would also be falling. There was a great deal of sliding and pawing and fancy hoofwork, but the Ovaro managed to regain his footing. Instead, Skye heard the snow-muffled thud as the dun gelding landed, and then its panicky scream that told of a snapped leg.

In that initial moment of turmoil, Fargo didn't hear the shooting. He saw the dim shape of the packhorse rear struggling almost on top of him and wrench aside as if hit, then go down again sprawling. Snow spouted up

against his face. He saw, then, the wicked flicker of ri.
muzzles, heard the blast of gunpowder. He scrambled t
his feet, crouching.

The Ovaro was still tromping dangerously, but it was a
case of shoot or be shot like a grazing buck. Fargo went
after his Sharps rifle in the saddle scabbard, tearing it
free with both hands. He fell to one knee, loaded and
capped the Sharps, and took aim. There were two guns
pitching lead out of the dark gloom of timber that flanked
the trail. One of the bullets slammed Fargo's hat sideways on his head. He shot at the flash, rechambered, and
shot again, then darted for the timber, not about to make
a permanent target of himself.

There was only darkness where one of the guns had
been firing.

Fargo heard a man's grunting curse, then the crunch of
boots running in the snow. He leapt after, straight into
the timber. Horses circled there, stamping fretfully in the
snow. Cold saddle leather strained protestingly. With
only the sounds to guide him, Fargo triggered out two
more bullets. One thudded into a tree; the other must
have been close or a hit, for at once the invisible
horse and rider went crashing wildly off through the
underbrush.

Gradually the racket faded in the hissing rush of the
snow. If Fargo was to have a look at the tracks, there
was no time to lose. By the light of sulfur matches struck
inside his coat, he headed for the spot where the horses
had been standing.

Halfway there, a huddled shape loomed against the
white snow. Fargo rolled the man over—he had a strag-
gling red beard and had been shot through the face.
Thirty feet farther along the mounts had been tied. One
was still there. Fargo ignored it while, shielding the square
match with a cupped hand, he studied for sign of the
ambusher who had escaped.

He found a good track where overhead branches had
kept off the snow. All four shoes were worn, the toes of
the hind pair being almost smooth; the off front hoof

∼ed in slightly—at some time or other that leg had been ∍adly bruised.

Lighting matches at intervals, Fargo pushed some two dozen paces along the track where the rider had plowed frantically off through the brush. All he found was a strip of dirty canvas some six inches long and two wide, impaled on the daggerlike end of a broken branch. Canvas storm coats were not uncommon. This strip had come from a sleeve, perhaps, as the arm slashed down with a quirt or the reins. He tucked it into his pocket and went back to the trail.

The packhorse's near foreleg had been broken just below the knee. Fargo would've had to shoot the poor animal, but the ambushers had already seen to that, and the dun gelding was dead. It took most of half an hour to free his pack and rope it on the dead ambusher's horse, a hock-torn dapple mare.

He had been too busy for emotion, but after he was riding on again, anger began to build within him. He'd been through trail trouble on his last job, when he'd brought a precocious orphan girl to her grandparents in Missoula. But having completed her delivery, he was now en route to Fort Walla Walla, where he'd heard there might be scouting or guide work available, and there was no reason for him to be attacked out here. And if those two bushwhackers hadn't been after him personally, they must've been the hungriest damn bandits in existence to have laid in wait for victims during a blizzard.

Bullshit. There had to be more of it than chance robbery.

Nothing could live long in the full stride of the storm, which was still rising. Snow raged howling out of the night, whipping his face raw and driving cold through to his bones. Hustled along by it, the weary Ovaro held to a lope. Fargo had given his mount his head, and was sitting forward in the saddle, hoping that the horse would take him to some draw where he could take shelter.

Abruptly his big black-and-white pinto halted dead in his tracks. Peering ahead, Fargo saw a bunch of steers, which had evidently drifted before the blizzard till they

struck a fence line. Now they were sullenly waiting wh
ever came. Some were already down.

Fargo slid out of the saddle and stumbled forward. He
could just make out the dark bulk of the individual
steers, but his groping fingers traced a brand on left
shoulder and flank.

"Star-bar," he muttered. "That's a new one on me."

Fighting his way back to the packhorse, which stood
with drooping head, Fargo fished out a new hemp lariat
he'd bought in Missoula. Tying one end to the fence and
snubbing the other end to his saddle horn, he spurred his
Ovaro and wrenched the rails down between two posts.
Then, recoiling his rope and stowing it back in his pack,
he began rousting the steers. After he had them all
lumbering through the gap in the fence, he got back into
his saddle and again gave the horse his head.

It must have been half an hour later, although Fargo
had lost all definite idea of time, that his horse topped a
ridge and came quartering down into a valley and again
halted. There was some kind of human shelter over there,
facing them. At first Fargo thought it was a cabin. Then
he saw that it was a dugout, built back into the sloping
face of a gully wall.

He didn't stop to pound on the door. It opened easily
to his push and the shove of the wind, and he stumbled
into an unlighted room. The air in here was warm, in
contrast to what he had just been through. Shutting the
door, he struck a match and saw a lantern hanging on a
peg driven into one sod wall. There were no windows. A
rusty cookstove, a homemade chair and table, and a
rough bunk, covered with blankets and hides, made up
the spartan furnishings. Whoever owned the dugout had
been away from home for some while, judging by the
dust and cobwebs over everything.

The Ovaro was pawing at the door. Fargo saw that he
couldn't get either horse through the low doorway. He
went outside and, with his gloved hands, groped till he
found one end of a tight-stretched wire about shoulder
high. Trailing the wire with his left hand, he led the

rses through the raging storm. The wind, striking them
om one side, made both horse and man stumble. But
he other end of the wire was pegged, as Fargo had
guessed, to the front of a second and larger dugout.
Blizzard wires were common and necessary in this part of
the hills. He led the horses inside, removed his riding
gear and pack, and was halfway back to the dugout when
he heard an eerie, wind-driven voice.

It wasn't the bawl of a steer, as Fargo, in the first
moment, had hoped. It was a man's voice, desperate and
exhausted.

T.G. HORNE—A SENSATIONAL
NEW WESTERN SERIES
BY PIERCE MACKENZIE

☐ **T.G. HORNE #1: THE STOLEN WHITE EAGLE.** T.G. Horne bet his life on the turn of a card of the draw of a gun as he roamed the West in search of high-stake gaming and no-limit loving. Now he was aboard the stolen *White Eagle*, playing showdown with Enoch Hardaway, a poker wizard who'd never been beat.... (147111—$2.50)

☐ **T.G. HORNE #2: THE FLEECING OF FODDER CITY.** With an ace up his sleeve and a gun in his hand, T.G. Horne headed for Fodder City where the action looked like a sure bet to him. The town was ripe with gold and women ripe for loving and Horne soon found himself down to his last chip and bullet in a game where ladies were wild and killers held all the cards.... (147138—$2.50)

☐ **T.G. HORNE #3: WINNER TAKE NOTHING.** T.G. Horne was tops at playing stud and never met a man he couldn't outdraw in either a poker game or a shootout, or a lady he couldn't impress with his hard loving. But now he was searching for a swindler who had played him for a sucker. And in a game of no chance he had all the dice and guns loaded against him.... (147847—$2.50)

☐ **T.G. HORNE #4: THE SPANISH MONTE FIASCO.** Horne thought that beating a bunch of Mexicans at their own game would be easy. But the cards were marked against him when he got caught in a trap with a Mexican spitfire. Here double-crossing father had *Horne* marked—and he had to stop drawing aces and start drawing guns. (148630—$2.50)
